Front page news?!?

Victoria settled on the couch and patted the cushion beside her. I sat obediently and waited.

"I probably should have showed this to you earlier, but I didn't know what to make of it," she said. "I picked it up at a convenience store this morning." She pulled a folded newspaper from her bag and spread it out on the table before us. "There," she said, pointing.

I just about fell off the couch.

I knew enough to recognize the format of a European tabloid. It's not like it's a serious newspaper or anything, more like the *National Enquirer* back home. But that picture was me! On the front page!

OTHER BOOKS YOU MAY ENJOY

LIGHTS, CAMERA, CASSIDY

episode one:
Celebrity

WITHDRAWN

by LINDA GERBER

PUFFIN BOOKS
An Imprint of Penguin Group (USA) Inc.

PUFFIN BOOKS

Published by the Penguin Group

Penguin Young Readers Group, 345 Hudson Street, New York, New York 10014, U.S.A.

Penguin Group (Canada), 90 Eglinton Avenue East, Suite 700, Toronto, Ontario, Canada M4P 2Y3
(a division of Pearson Penguin Canada Inc.)

Penguin Books Ltd, 80 Strand, London WC2R 0RL, England

Penguin Ireland, 25 St Stephen's Green, Dublin 2, Ireland (a division of Penguin Books Ltd)

Penguin Group (Australia), 250 Camberwell Road, Camberwell, Victoria 3124, Australia
(a division of Pearson Australia Group Pty Ltd)

Penguin Books India Pvt Ltd, 11 Community Centre,
Panchsheel Park, New Delhi - 110 017, India

Penguin Group (NZ), 67 Apollo Drive, Rosedale, Auckland 0632, New Zealand
(a division of Pearson New Zealand Ltd)

Penguin Books (South Africa) (Pty) Ltd, 24 Sturdee Avenue,
Rosebank, Johannesburg 2196, South Africa

Registered Offices: Penguin Books Ltd, 80 Strand, London WC2R 0RL, England

Published by Puffin Books, a division of Penguin Young Readers Group, 2012

1 3 5 7 9 10 8 6 4 2

LIBRARY OF CONGRESS CATALOGING-IN-PUBLICATION DATA IS AVAILABLE

Puffin Books ISBN 978-0-14-241814-7

Design by Theresa Evangelista
Text set in Adobe Caslon

Printed in the United States of America

For Haley, my Cassidy muse

ACKNOWLEDGMENTS: Special thanks to Elaine Spencer for making it happen; to Kristin Gilson for her guidance; to Tricia Cowan and Sally Cutting for their Spain expertise; to Aisling, Christella, and David for their Irish input; to Luisa Chu for her travel show wisdom; and to Theresa Evangelista for another awesome cover!

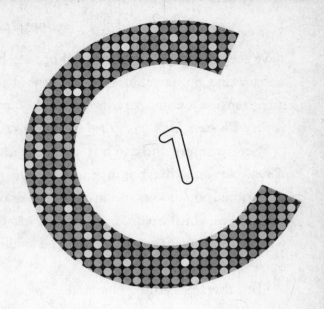

I like a challenge.

My grampa used to say my determination was something that could get me far in life. What he didn't say was that it could also get me in trouble.

I found out just how much trouble the night I snuck out of our apartment in Spain.

The tabloids have printed at least a hundred different versions of what happened next. Some of the stories are true. Most of them, not so much. I still have to laugh that the papers ran them at all.

I mean, since when am *I* news? First of all, I'm only twelve (almost thirteen). Second, before Spain, hardly anyone even knew who I was. No, I take that back. They might have seen my picture on one of those celebrity shows or in a magazine, but never just as me. I was always an accessory, an extension of my parents—*Cassidy Barnett, daughter of reality TV stars Julia and Davidson Barnett.*

See, my mom and dad host a travel show called *When in Rome*. Not only that, but my mom has written about ten international cookbooks and my dad has his own line of travel accessories. Until Spain, my only job was to jet around the world with them, watching from the sideline. Hardly anyone ever noticed me.

But then everything changed.

What happened that first morning wasn't my fault. Well, okay, it sort of was, but none of it would have happened if the airline hadn't lost my suitcase, so at least partial blame belongs to them.

The way I see it, I wouldn't have had to sneak out if I could have set up my room properly. I'm not talking about full-on decor or anything, just a few things I bring with me when we travel. We move around with the show so much that I could easily end up sleeping in a strange bed in a strange room every few weeks. Having my stuff set up helps make each room feel like *mine.*

I have a brass incense burner I bought in India, a string of star-shaped twinkling lights from France, a fuzzy Japanese Hello Kitty pillow, and—most importantly—a framed picture of my grampa and me that was taken at his farm in Ohio.

That picture was the last one we ever had taken together. We're sitting on the creaky old porch swing in front of his house, and Grampa's smiling straight into the camera like he knows he's going to be looking out at me from the other side. I can almost hear him telling me, "Wherever you go, Cassie, I'll be there with you."

But he wasn't there that first morning in Valencia, all because of the stupid airline.

It was still dark outside when I woke up. At first, everything was fine. I lay in bed and listened to the pipes knocking in the walls, imagining all the places we were going to visit for the show that day.

Then I remembered. I had no suitcase. The cute new sundress I'd bought to wear for my first day in Spain was lost in some airport somewhere. Worse, without my things, my room felt empty. Empty. EMPTY.

I switched on the lamp to chase away the shadows, but—even with its authentic Mediterranean touches—the room looked even bleaker in the light . . . like a really well-furnished cell. The air smelled stale. The closeness of the walls made my skin itch. I couldn't stand it. I had to get *out*. Out of the room, out of the apartment, out of the building so I could breathe again.

The problem was, my mom and dad were still asleep, and it would have been rude to wake them up just to ask for permission, right? I wasn't going to go far. Maybe just walk around our temporary neighborhood a little bit. Explore the surroundings. We were staying right in the middle of the historic district, so I could probably get some good pictures for my blog—even if it was still kind of dark.

Did I mention it was four in the morning?

The early hour would make slipping out a little tricky. My mom and dad's bedroom was right across the hall from mine. Plus, there was a doorman on duty down in the lobby who might ask questions. But as I said, I like a challenge. I figured I was up for it.

That was my first mistake.

Getting out of the apartment was easy. My mom and dad aren't exactly known for being light sleepers. Which was good because my dad snores loud enough to drown out a 747. They probably didn't even hear me tiptoe past their room and out the front door of the apartment.

Sneaking down to the lobby was the tricky part. The elevator was one of those really old cagelike things that rattled and groaned whenever it went up and down. If I didn't want to wake up everyone in the building, I had to take the stairs, and that meant I had zero chance of getting past the doorman unnoticed. The staircase emptied out right in front of his desk.

Sure enough, I got only about halfway down the steps before he glanced up from the soccer game he was watching on the small television at his desk. From his bland expression, I couldn't tell if he recognized me or not. Like I said, my mom and dad were the television stars. I was just a footnote. But he had to know I belonged with the Americans who had arrived that night. If he wanted to rat me out, he'd know exactly who to buzz, so I had to make sure he didn't think there was a reason to rat.

I gave him my best celebrity smile and practically sang "Good morning!" as I bounced down the rest of the stairs.

"Buenos días," he replied, but he didn't smile back. His heavy black eyebrows huddled together like he was unsure what he was supposed to do next. He kind of half stood, stooped over, like a question mark hanging in the air.

I pointed to myself and then to the revolving glass front door. "Going running."

His face relaxed, and he settled back into his seat like I figured he would.

See, the thing about most grown-ups is that they would rather not know if something's wrong because then they have to deal with it. So as long as I acted like it was perfectly normal for someone my age to go out running alone before the sun came up, it was a pretty good bet he wouldn't bother me. Or alert my mom and dad. Or notice that I was wearing purple Converse high-tops, not running shoes.

I breezed through the lobby, waving good-bye to the

doorman as I passed his desk, but he had already turned back to his game.

Once I was safely outside and down the block—out of sight of the apartment building—I paused to pull my cell phone and earbuds from my pocket. I quickly put together a playlist of Spanish music that ran exactly thirty-four minutes. That way, when I got to the last song, I would know it was time to turn back. Just to be safe, I also set the phone's alarm so I'd be sure to make it to the apartment before the time Mom and Dad usually woke up.

After all that, I finally relaxed. I closed my eyes and took a deep breath, savoring the smell of freedom and Valencia. I know that probably sounds weird, but every city has its own smell—especially in the morning before it gets buried under exhaust fumes and heat. In Valencia it was a combination of concrete and oranges and fresh-cut grass, with a faint, salty sea tang that drifted in with the mist from the ocean. I made a mental note of it, and set off to find some pictures to post as well.

I started my blog when my grampa first got sick. Because his medicine made him feel tired a lot, he had to stop driving and he couldn't do as much around the farm as he used to. I hated that while my mom and dad and I were off seeing the world with the show, his world was shrinking. Gramma finally got wireless at the house and bought him a laptop so he could sit out on the porch and still be able to get online. It helped for him to have something to keep his mind occupied, she said.

I had just gotten a new cell phone with a camera from my mom and dad for my birthday, so I decided to keep a photo diary of our travels for Grampa. That way he'd have some kind of connection with us whenever he got online. I wrote him notes and took pictures I thought would make him laugh. Like Dad asleep on the plane with a big string of drool hanging from his mouth. Or Mom prepping for a segment with rollers in her hair and the makeup tissue tucked into her collar.

When Grampa died, I kept the blog going. It made me feel like I was still connected to him in a way. I continued to send him messages and talk to him as if he was with me. I kept looking for things I knew would make him smile.

It didn't take long before fans of my mom and dad's show discovered my blog. When the *When in Rome* producers saw how many followers I was getting, they offered to host my blog on their website. They even bought me a nicer cell phone with a better camera—this one with video. That should have been my first clue that the blog wasn't just about Grampa anymore.

Within weeks, my hundreds of followers turned into thousands. Mom and Dad weren't thrilled to have so many strangers following me, even if most of those followers were fans of the show. After a long discussion with the network, it was decided I could keep blogging as long as I followed a strict list of guidelines, which included disabling the comments. The last thing my mom and dad wanted was some creeper talking to me online.

So anyway, that's how it all started. I'll admit that when I snuck out that morning, it did occur to me that just in case I wound up getting caught, my mom and dad might go easier on me if I could say I'd done it all for the blog. Proves how much I know.

Our apartment building sat across the street from the Plaza de la Reina, which put us within walking distance of everything in Old Town—the Turia Fountain, the basilica, and the Valencia Cathedral with its *miguelete* tower.

I wandered through the historic district, mostly just getting background images that I would edit later when I wrote about our first day in Spain.

Hardly anyone was out that morning, only a few cars going through the roundabout and maybe a delivery truck or two. It was peaceful and quiet as I walked along—just me and my camera and the music.

The last song in my playlist was just ending as I reached the Plaza de la Virgen. I checked the time. Close. I quickly tucked away the earbuds and set the camera to video. The plaza had its own music in the sloshing of the fountain and a quartet of birds too impatient to wait for dawn. It was the perfect sound track for a quick vlog message to go along with all the images I'd been filming.

I propped my phone on the edge of the fountain, making the Door of the Apostles and the Valencia Cathedral my backdrop, and took a few steps back.

"Buenos días, Abuelo," I said to the camera. "That means 'Good morning, Grampa.' We got to Spain late last night, but—"

Just then my phone started to vibrate, buzzing and skipping over the stones toward the pool of the fountain.

"Crap!" I jumped and managed to grab the phone right before it fell into the water. My heart felt like it was going to pound its way right out of my chest. The alarm meant I had to get back to the apartment. Fast.

I held the phone at arm's length and finished quickly. "I've got to run, but I'll give you an update later. *¡Nos vemos pronto!* That's Spanish for 'See you soon.' *¡Adios!*"

The doorman was standing behind his desk when I rushed back into the lobby. He'd been talking on the phone, but he cut it short and set down the receiver when he saw me. His little television wasn't on anymore.

Oh, crap, I thought. *He knows I snuck out.*

Dread clawed at me every step up the staircase to our apartment. If the door guy knew I wasn't supposed to be out on my own, someone must have told him. Someone like my mom and dad. They were probably waiting for me on the landing, ready to lock me in my room. I trudged even slower.

The door to our apartment was silent and closed, just the way I'd left it. Maybe all wasn't lost. I pulled the key from my pocket and reached for the door when a shape stepped out from the shadows.

"Oooh. You're in trouble."

2

One of the cool things about traveling around the world with a television crew is that it's almost like having family everywhere we go. Our fixer, Bayani, has been with the show since the first season, so he's like a big brother to me. A really loud, obnoxious big brother who thinks it's funny to jump out and scare me at five in the morning. He's twenty-five, but with his shaggy black hair and lanky build, he doesn't look that much older than me. He doesn't act that much older, either.

I slugged his arm. "Don't *do* that!"

He just grinned. "Where've you been?"

"Shhh!" I hissed. "Quiet."

"Not gonna help." Bayani shook his head. "You're hosed."

"Hosed? Seriously? No one says that anymore."

He laughed, and I had to shush him again.

"When did they find out I was gone?" I whispered.

"Not sure." He didn't even bother to keep his voice down. "Ten minutes ago, maybe? That's when they woke me up to join the search. You should get inside. They're about ready to send out the *caballeria*."

"The what?"

He rolled his eyes. "The cavalry, Cass."

"How would I know that?"

"Pretty obvious from the context."

"Yeah? Well, I'm sorry I didn't—"

"Cassidy." Dad's angry voice cut me off. "Inside. Now."

My stomach sank right to the tiled floor. I turned slowly. He was standing in the doorway, arms folded tightly across his chest. Mom stood right behind him. Both of their faces were puckered and pinchy, like they'd eaten bad kumquats or something.

Beside me, Bayani took a step back, as if the trouble I was in might be contagious. "I'll, uh . . . yeah. Later." He turned and retreated down the stairs.

I had no choice but to trudge into the apartment alone while Mom and Dad glared white-hot daggers at me. That's what it felt like, anyway. Dad ordered me into the front room and pointed to the couch. He told me to sit. I sank onto the sleek leather and they towered over me.

Mom spoke first.

"Just where have you been?"

One of the many annoying things about parents is that they ask questions when they really don't want to know the answers. I started to explain about why I had to get out of my room that morning, but Mom just shook her head, too angry to listen.

"What were you thinking," she demanded, "wandering alone at night?"

"It's morning," I mumbled.

"Excuse me?"

I studied the pattern of the rug at my feet. "Nothing."

"It's *not* morning," she said tightly, "until the sun comes up."

"What?" I knew it would have been smarter to keep my mouth shut, but you know how I said I love a challenge? I couldn't help myself. "That doesn't even make sense."

"Cassidy," Dad warned, "backtalk will not help your situation."

"But, Dad, she said—"

"The point is"—Mom's voice rose an octave—"you know better than to go wandering away without permission. You had us worried sick. We were about to call the police."

Wow. Talk about overreacting. "I wasn't wandering," I argued. "I just wanted to see what—"

"You could have been hurt," Dad said. "Or worse."

I folded my arms and slumped back against the couch. Traitor. Of anyone, I thought Dad would understand. He's the one who was always telling me to "think for myself" and to "explore my surroundings."

Mom sat down beside me, her hands pressed tightly together in her lap. "It may be," she said slowly, "that the time has come to make a change." Her voice had gone soft and apologetic, and that scared me even more than the anger. I didn't know how it happened, but her tone told me the conversation had just taken a sharp left turn.

My throat squeezed tight. "What kind of change?"

I had to ask, even though I already knew the answer. I mean, I overhear stuff. It's kind of hard not to when we spend so much time together in small spaces. My mom and dad are so used to tuning out the cameras, the crowds, and the crew when they're working; sometimes they forget and tune me out, too. So they talk. I know they've been wondering if maybe it would be better for me in a "normal" home with friends my age, regular school, blah, blah, blah. I always figured they were just talking, but now . . .

Mom gave me this weird, sad little smile and tucked a strand of my hair behind my ear. I shook it back out, and she sighed. "Your father and I have been thinking," she said, slipping a quick, meaningful look up to where my dad still stood. I knew right then I wasn't going to like what they'd been thinking about. "You're almost a teenager now. Perhaps you need—"

Don't say it. Don't say it.

"—a more structured environment."

I stared at her. Was she kidding? She always said structure was for the unimaginative. "What are you saying?"

Dad sat on the other side of me and rested his hand on my shoulder like we were suddenly best friends. "We think it might be good for you to take a break from the show for a while. Your grandmother said you're welcome to stay as long as you li—"

I jerked away from him. "You want to dump me with Gramma?"

His face crumpled like I'd just swiped his lollipop. "You like visiting Gramma."

"Yeah. *Visiting*, not staying."

Before you get the wrong idea, I should tell you—I love my gramma. I really do. We've always stayed at her farm on breaks and between shows, so it's the closest thing to home I know. But that's just it. It's *her* place now. It used to be hers and Grampa's, but now he's gone. I don't like going to the farm anymore. It hurts too much to be there without him.

But Dad didn't understand that. He kept talking like I was supposed to be excited they had worked out all these details without ever mentioning it to me. "We thought it might be nice for you to attend regular school for a change," he said. "Get involved. Make new friends."

"My friends are here. With the show."

"I'm talking about friends your age." Dad said. "You remember that little neighbor girl, Kristy? You could have her introduce you around . . ."

There was more, but I stopped listening. I told you he didn't understand. My gramma's neighbor's granddaughter was Christine, not Kristy, and I hadn't talked to her for at least a year. She stopped coming around the first time she saw my picture with Mom and Dad on the cover of *TV Guide*. She said I wasn't as special as I thought I was. I told her she was just jealous. Grampa made me apologize, but I never saw her again after that.

Except for Christine and her little brother, who was supremely annoying, I didn't know any other kids in the school district. It was kind of hard to be sociable when all the farms are at least a mile apart and I was there only for weeks at a time. The last thing I wanted to do was to go to a school where everyone else knew one another and my only "friend" thought I was a stuck-up snob.

It's not like I'm a baby or anything. I've been to twenty-seven different countries. I've climbed mountains and pyramids. I can eat chicken feet and goat eyeballs without hurling. But the thought of sitting alone at a lunch table in some school cafeteria makes my stomach turn cold.

And, yeah, I know what I said about challenges. But I like to *choose* my challenges. Could I make it through a day of middle school? Yes. Did I *want* to? No way. But Mom and Dad had already made up their minds. Which was completely unfair.

"What about Victoria?" I asked. If they didn't care about me, they should at least think about her. Victoria was my tutor. She traveled with us to all our locations and made sure I stayed current with my schoolwork. If I started going to a regular school, Victoria would be out of a job. "What is she supposed to do?"

"Victoria will be fine," Dad assured me.

"But—"

"Your father and I only want what's best for you, Cassidy," Mom broke in. "We want you to be happy."

"Then why don't you ask me what I want?"

"This is not the first time we've spoken to you about wandering off, Cassidy." All the softness was gone from her voice. From her face, too. "You had us so worried! I'd put you on a plane right now just to keep you in one place, but—"

"No! Wait. Give me another chance. I promise I'll do better!" I hated to beg, but I was desperate. I would have gotten down on my knees if I thought it would do any good.

"I don't know, Cass," Dad said. He was starting to cave; I could feel it. So I directed my arguments to him.

"You always said this show was a family project. How can we be a family if I'm in Ohio and you're on the other side of the world?"

Dad exchanged another one of those looks with Mom, and then she pinched her lips together. She knew when she was beat. "You will remain with us for this shoot, Cassidy. But beyond that, the choice is up to you. We'll be watching . . ."

Travel tip: Always pack a change of clothes and some toiletries in your carry-on in case *you* make it to your destination but your luggage *doesn't*.

Mom made us eat breakfast together, even though I kept telling her I wasn't hungry. But after my family togetherness argument, how could I refuse? They were "watching," Mom said, so I made jokes with my dad and ate all the food on my plate and did everything I could to show them I was going to be a cheerful, obedient new me. Then I excused myself and escaped to my room. I love my parents, but all that cheer was making my cheeks hurt.

The airline still hadn't found my suitcase, which meant I had no clean clothes to wear except the T-shirt and boyfriend shorts I had carried in my backpack in case of emergency.

Being stranded in Spain with one change of clothes wasn't the worst thing in the world—I could always use an excuse to go shopping—but I missed having Grampa's picture to talk to. I needed him. Especially now that I was on probation.

At least I had my lucky charm necklace. I pulled the leather cord out from under my shirt and laid the necklace gently on top, my fingers searching the charms for the squiggly gold Italian *cornicello*. That was the first charm I'd ever gotten. Grampa had given it to me when I started traveling with Mom and Dad. He slipped the necklace over my head, making me promise never to take it off. The *cornicello* was for luck, he'd said. It would protect me as long as I stayed on the right path.

After that, charms became a "thing" with Grampa and me. Everywhere I traveled, I would find a new charm for the necklace, and when we got back to Ohio, he would tie it onto the cord for me. After he died, I kept the tradition going, even though tying on the charms by myself wasn't quite as meaningful. The *cornicello* would always be my favorite.

The apartment doorbell chimed. Probably Bayani. He was supposed to go over the shooting schedule for the next couple of days with Mom and Dad, and I wanted to see what was coming up, too. I hurried and smoothed the hem of my T-shirt, checking my reflection in the dresser mirror to make sure I didn't look too rumpled. Backpacks aren't known for their wrinkle-free effect on clothes.

I pulled the clip from my hair, and it tumbled down around my shoulders in honey-blond waves. Usually I wear my hair straight, but since my blow dryer and straightener were lost along with my suitcase, I had just scrunched it up into a messy bun after my shower and let it dry by itself. I was planning on combing it back into a ponytail, but I decided not to. People are always telling me how much I look like my mom with my blond hair and blue eyes, but her hair is always sleek and straight. This way I looked a little less like a mini-her. I liked that.

Except . . . I gasped and leaned closer to the mirror, lifting my bangs. A huge zit had erupted overnight, right in the middle of my forehead. Not cool. I brushed my bangs forward again to cover it up, but I could still see it. Maybe if I fluffed them a little. Or brushed them to the side. Or—

"Knock-knock."

I jumped away from the mirror just as Victoria swung the door open.

"Well! Don't you look nice?" She stepped behind me and smiled at me through the mirror. I always liked the way Victoria smiled. And the kindness in her eyes. And her thick, black hair that didn't need a straightener. But most of all I liked how she always seemed to be interested in how I felt and what I had to say.

Not like Mom and Dad, who were ready to ship me off to Ohio against my will.

Victoria stepped back. "Hey, now. What's with the frown? Let's have a look at you."

I turned from the mirror and gave her an exaggerated curtsy. "Like it? It's the very latest in backpack couture."

"Very fashionable. Lovely the way your shoes pick up the purple in your shirt."

"Oh, yeah." I turned back to the mirror. "Not planned. I wanted to wear sandals."

"Well, those look cute with your shorts. And I like how your charms add just a touch of sparkle."

I fingered the *cornicello* again, and my smile returned. Victoria always did know how to make me feel better.

She hooked her arm through mine. "Come along, then. Your mum and dad are ready to go over the shoot schedule."

When we walked into the kitchen, Bayani was already going over the details of the schedule with Mom and Dad. He glanced up and didn't even bother hiding his smile. "Oh, look. You're still alive."

"Ha, ha."

"Have a seat," he said. "You'll want to hear some of this, too."

I pulled out a chair. "Where's Cavin?" I asked. Cavin was our director, and he usually ran the planning meetings.

"Flight's been delayed," Dad said. "We'll have to start without him."

Bayani handed me one of the schedule sheets. "Think you can follow along?"

I didn't even dignify that with an answer. I tuned out Bayani and skimmed over the highlights on the paper. Today we'd be mostly shooting B-roll footage. That's the kind of background filler stuff you see on shows between scenes that are supposed to give a sense of time or place. Since *When in Rome* is a travel show, they use a lot of B-roll, sometimes with a voice-over, telling about the area. I liked B-roll days because everyone was pretty laid-back, and sometimes the crew even let me get behind the camera or hold the boom mike so I would have something to talk about on my blog. One show segment was scheduled with my mom later in the afternoon, but the rest of the time looked like fun.

In the evening, we'd catch the train to Buñol, where we would take part in the Tomatina (Tomato) Festival the next day.

My eyes kind of glassed over after that. Too many details on the page. All I wanted to know was what we were going to see, and would there be any shopping. Of course, as the fixer, Bayani had to go over every detail with Mom and Dad at least four times each.

A fixer's the person who goes to the location ahead of the rest of the crew and arranges everything. He finds the local guides, checks out venues and filming locations, and makes sure everything runs smoothly at each shoot. The network had hired Bayani as the local fixer in the Philippines, and they liked him so much, he stayed on with the crew. He's as good at his job as he is at teasing—and that's saying a lot.

"Hello?" Bayani flicked my paper so that it fluttered out of my hand and onto the table. "Are you listening? Some of these locations today were set up especially with you and—"

Dad suddenly had a coughing fit and waved Bayani's paper away. "We, er, haven't had a chance to discuss that yet."

They had my full attention now. "Discuss what?"

"We've, uh . . . we've had to make a few changes of assignment this trip," Dad said.

"Right," Bayani agreed. "The network would like to see more of—"

Dad shook his head to cut Bayani short. "The thing is, with Cavin's delay, Bayani will be taking on some of the director's duties, and . . . let's see . . ." He glanced down at the papers he held in his hand and nodded. "Jack, it appears, had a family matter to attend to, so we are short one cameraman and we'll have to make a substitution."

Not exactly big news. Since we traveled with a small crew, everyone took on extra duties from time to time. Bayani, for example, also handled a camera. And Victoria often helped with the editing. None of which had anything to do with me. "No, really," I said, "what do we need to discuss?"

Mom turned so that she was facing me, one arm resting casually across the back of her chair. Too casually, I thought. "We've had a request from the network," she said.

I didn't like how cheerful she sounded all of a sudden. It made me feel like I was being set up for something. I slid a look to Victoria for help. She could usually fill me in on all the crew gossip, but she just shook her head and shrugged.

"It's the ratings war," Dad said. "We're falling behind." For years, *When in Rome* and a rival show, *A Foreign Affair*, had been competing for everything from numbers to sponsors to time slots. This was the first time I ever heard of *A Foreign Affair* pulling ahead.

"Okay," I said cautiously. I mean, I was sorry to hear about it and all, but again, I wasn't sure what it had to do with me.

"The network feels," Mom said, "that we might bolster our ratings by trying to reach a younger demographic. They've noted the increasing number of hits on your blog and suggested we include you in the B-roll footage."

"Really?" I just about jumped out of my seat. I mean, it's not like she was talking about giving me a segment or anything, but getting onto the show was big. At least to me. I'd been begging for a chance to get on camera for months. "What do I get to do? Can we do beach shots, please? *Please?*"

"Not on the itinerary for today," Bayani said, tapping my paper again. "But don't worry, there'll be plenty of candid shots waiting for you and—"

Dad started up with his coughing fit again. What was

his problem? Inserting me into the setting sounded simple enough, so why was Dad all nervous about "discussing" it with me? I wanted to know what Bayani was about to say when Dad cut him off. Me and . . . and what?

"You remember me telling you about my old friend Hector?" Dad asked.

"Um, yeah." Only about a million times. Dad had met Hector Ruiz-Moreno when they were both part of an international studies program at the University of London. Now Señor Ruiz-Moreno was a professor of anthropology at the Universidad Politècnia de Valencia, and he was going to be our guide this trip. Again, what did that have to do with me?

Dad straightened the napkin next to his plate, smiling to himself. "Back in college, Hector and I—"

"'Hitchhiked from Paris to Prague on a dollar a day,'" I quoted. It's all he'd been talking about for weeks.

Someone knocked on the door, and my mom sat a little taller. "Well. That must be them."

Dad jumped out of his chair and hurried to answer the door. Mom followed, smoothing a hand over her hair.

"What's going on?" I whispered to Victoria.

She watched them curiously. "I've no idea. Let's go find out, shall we?"

In the front hall I stopped dead and stared at the man Dad was clapping on the back. Not some old professorial type with thick glasses and a pocket protector like I'd imagined. No way. This guy looked like Antonio Banderas. I'm not even kidding. My dad used to hang out with *him*?

Mom must have sensed me staring because she turned and said, "Ah. There she is!" She waved me over. "Come here, Cassidy. We'd like you to meet someone. This," she said proudly, "is Hector Ruiz-Moreno."

Travel tip: When greeting locals in Spain, it's customary to . . .

Oh, man. I didn't know. My mind had gone completely blank. I just stood there like an idiot staring at Señor Ruiz-Moreno, trying to remember if I was supposed to bow or shake his hand or—

He reached out and grabbed me by the shoulders and kissed me on both cheeks. Oh. Right. That was it.

"*Encantado*, Cassidy," he said. "I have heard much about you."

"Oh . . ." I replied.

"And this," Mom continued, "is Hector's son, Mateo." She stepped back to reveal the guy standing just behind Señor Ruiz-Moreno. He had earbuds in his ears and was looking off into the distance, his head bobbing to whatever was playing on his iPod.

Señor Ruiz-Moreno cleared his throat and said something in rapid Spanish I didn't understand. Mateo startled and quickly pulled out the earbuds. Señor Ruiz-Moreno nodded pointedly at my mom and dad and me.

"*Lo siento*," Mateo said. "I am sorry."

"My son," Señor Ruiz-Moreno said. I couldn't tell by his tone if the announcement was supposed to be proud or apologetic, but to be honest with you, I really didn't care. I was too busy trying not to be obvious about staring.

Judging from his clothes and the angles of his face, Mateo was probably about my age. He had black wavy hair like his dad, but it was cut shorter. His skin was tan like creamed caramel, and just as smooth. He looked at me with deep brown eyes framed by eyelashes so dark, it almost looked like he was wearing guyliner. When he smiled, I had to fight an insane urge to giggle.

"Nice to meet you," I said.

"And you," he replied.

He took a step forward, and my mouth went dry. For an instant I wondered if he was going to kiss me on both cheeks like his dad had. The thought made me feel all giddy inside. And nervous. I quickly smoothed down my bangs to make sure the zit was covered and wondered if I should lean in to make the kissing easier. Or would that be too obvious? Maybe I should just—

Mateo took my hand in his and shook it. Oh. I tried not

to let my disappointment show. On the other hand, I really had enjoyed the press of his hand against mine . . .

"We thought it might be nice if Hector brought Mateo along with us as we tour Valencia," Dad said, "so you'd have someone your own age to visit with."

My previous thoughts of handshakes and cheek kissing crashed down around me. Really, Dad? *My own age?* And then it made sense. Bayani's comment. Dad's reluctance to tell me the truth.

The heat in my face flared. I couldn't believe it. Here I was, almost thirteen years old, and my parents were setting me up on a playdate!

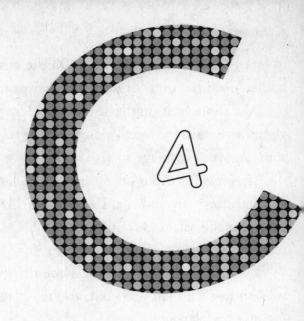

Bayani joined us all at the door.

He was in full director mode with a clipboard in his hands and his lucky Yankees cap turned backward on his head. "Well, good. Now that everyone's here, let's head on down. The rest of the crew should be waiting in the lobby by now."

I was grateful for the distraction; it gave me a moment to pull myself together. I don't have a whole lot of practice making conversation with (way cute!) boys my age. What was I supposed to say to him for an entire day? How was I supposed to act?

In case you're wondering if I'd ever met a boy before, let me clear that up for you. I have. I meet lots of boys when we travel. But I don't *hang out* with them.

It's not like I'm a social outcast. Victoria makes sure I know the etiquette for each country we visit. I can appropriately greet royalty and heads of state, no problem. But most of the people we meet are old, like my mom and dad.

I was on the verge of full-on panic until I noticed the way my mom was watching me. Gauging my reaction. And suddenly everything made annoying sense.

I'd put you on a plane right now to keep you in one place, she'd said, *but . . .*

But When in Rome's ratings were slipping. *But* the network wanted to reach younger viewers. *But* they'd already arranged for Mateo to join us. *But* I could be useful to the show.

I wasn't sure whether to be relieved or angry. My own parents were using me!

On the other hand . . . this gave me a chance to get in front of the cameras for a change, just like I wanted. Besides—I stole another peek at Mateo—the company wasn't bad. At all. It didn't take a genius to figure out that as long as I was an asset to the show, they couldn't send me home. So I'd just have to make sure to stay useful. And keep out of trouble. That shouldn't be too hard, right?

Mateo glanced up while I was looking at him, and for an instant I caught the shadow of a frown before he turned on the smile again. (And can I just say, he has a *very* nice smile.) I understood in that moment that Mateo must feel as uncomfortable about the forced arrangement as I did. His dad probably dragged him into this the same way mine had.

"I'm sorry," I mouthed.

He looked surprised for a moment. "It's okay," he mouthed back, and then smiled even broader.

Did I mention the nice smile?

By then, the old people moved off in a cluster, and I was left standing with Mateo, trying to think of something to say. "You speak English really well," I blurted. Lame, I know.

"Thanks," he said, grinning. "So do you."

Okay. I deserved that. "Yes, but *I* don't speak Spanish."

"Catalan," he corrected. "Or Valencian, depending on where we are."

"Oh. Right." I forgot how Victoria said the Spaniards are very particular about their language. Spanish is something that can be spoken anywhere. Like in Mexico or Venezuela. Catalan was spoken in most of Spain. In the Valencia region, they might also use Valencian.

"We lived in London when I was younger," Mateo explained, "so I grew up speaking English."

Bayani waved us over. "Hey," he called, "none of that sneaking-off-together stuff. This is a family show."

The burning in my face returned. "He's a dead man," I swore to myself. And then I turned to apologize to Mateo again. "Sorry. He thinks he's funny."

★ **Celebrity** ★   33

"*Está bien*," Mateo said. "It is fine. I like to see what it's truly like for the people behind the scenes."

"Oh, so you've seen my mom and dad's show?"

He grinned at me sheepishly. "Actually, no. My father watches it, though."

"Oh. Well, I'm sorry you got dragged into this. Since our dads are friends, they probably thought we'd . . . um . . ."

"Get along?" Mateo offered.

"Yeah." I wished I knew a way to stop my cheeks from combusting every time I opened my mouth.

"I don't mind."

"Really?" I asked.

"Sure. It could be fun."

I watched his eyes when he said that. He seemed sincere. The idea that he might actually want to hang out with me made me go warm inside. Maybe, I thought, a playdate wasn't such a bad thing after all.

We met up with the rest of the crew downstairs in the lobby. Bayani was filling them in on the day's schedule.

"I'm sorry, but I don't know how this works," Mateo whispered. "What are we doing?"

"Everyone needs to know how to prepare for the day," I said. "Which locations need lighting, where we'll need sound, that kind of thing. Today we're mostly filming background stuff. Only one segment scheduled, and that's not until this afternoon."

"What are segments?"

"Those are like the meat of the show. Usually some kind of interview or demonstration or something. Today my mom's segment will be talking about your *horchata* drink."

"Ah." He nodded. "Will we watch that? My dad likes the food parts best."

"Really? I won't tell my dad. He'll be bummed."

Mateo looked confused, so I explained. "Mom does all the food segments. Dad does most of the culture bits and some of the voice-overs. He likes to think everyone likes his segments best."

"And what do you do?"

I pointed back to where the tech guys were fitting my mom with her wireless mic, clipping it onto her lapel. "Usually I'm with them, behind the cameras. Sometimes I film what's going on for my blog."

"Yes, I've seen it," he said.

I couldn't help smiling. "My blog? Really? You have?"

He nodded and looked at me from under those dark lashes. "When my dad told me we'd be meeting you this week, I . . . I looked you up online."

"You actually did a search on me? I'm flattered."

I must have been talking a little too loud because Bayani shot me a look. "This evening," he said pointedly, raising his voice and snapping the schedule in his hand, "we will travel to Buñol to film a segment at the Tomatina Festival's paella cook-off. Tomorrow is the festival itself. Friday is the segment at the Mercado Central, and on Saturday . . ."

"Is he going to go through the whole three weeks?" Mateo whispered.

"Man, I hope not. That would be—"

"Cassidy!" Bayani interrupted. "Would you mind keeping it down? I'd rather not have to repeat myself."

I shot him a look and pulled an imaginary zipper across my lips. Jeez. Give some people a drop of authority, and it goes straight to their heads. I was about to say something to Mateo about it when I noticed my mom looking at me. I quickly closed my mouth and tried to look interested in what Bayani was saying.

By then, he was pointing to our big teddy bear of a makeup artist. "Daniel will be standing in behind camera two for Jack, who couldn't make this trip."

Daniel stepped forward and waved to us like he was an Olympic competitor greeting his fans.

"This ought to be interesting," I whispered to Mateo.

"And finally," Bayani continued, "Cavin won't be here until this afternoon, so in case you haven't noticed, I'm filling in for him. You have any questions, you can come to me."

Mateo leaned closer. "Who's Cavin?"

"He's the executive director," I whispered. "He's flying in from Ireland, but his flight was delayed." Cavin was usually our go-between with the network. I wondered if he knew about the plans to inject Mateo and me into the show. If anything, it was probably his idea.

"One last thing," Bayani said. "We're missing some equipment courtesy of the airline, so we'll be using rentals and paying by the hour. Let's make every shot count!"

Everyone split up after that, like they were breaking from a huddle. I was about to take Mateo around and introduce him to everyone when Victoria stepped up behind us. "You're next with Daniel," she said, pointing to where our makeup man was pushing through the revolving door with his kit in one hand and a folding stool tucked under his arm.

"Where's he going?" Mateo asked.

"We're filming outdoors today," I told him, "so he'll want to do our makeup outside to get the right lighting."

Mateo stepped back. "Makeup? I don't think so."

"Relax," I said, trying to hide my grin as I echoed his words from earlier. "It could be fun."

Travel tip: Spain in August is hot!

Don't forget the sunscreen.

Walking outside from the air-conditioned lobby was like stepping into a sauna. It was only nine in the morning, but already the sun was beating down mercilessly. I was amazed at how much hotter it was than when I'd been out earlier.

"Over here," Daniel called. He had set up the chair right in the middle of the sidewalk where everyone could see him powder our shine. Awkward.

A few curious people were already standing around, watching what was going on. That wasn't unusual. Cameras typically attract attention. It didn't faze me when I was part of the crew, but now I was the one on display. Part of me got a secret thrill out of it. I mean, who wouldn't want to feel like a star, right? But the other part of me was really nervous that I was going to do something completely stupid in front of everyone. And have it caught on tape.

Daniel motioned for me to sit down, and Mateo watched from the shade under the awning. "Loving the hair," Daniel said, fluffing the ends with his fingers. "Very smart leaving it natural for today. I'm afraid those bangs might blow into your eyes, though, so why don't we pull them back with a headband and—"

Before I could stop him, he started to brush the hair from my forehead. I jerked back, but he was quicker.

"Oh, my," he said when he saw the zit. "Let's go with the bangs down, shall we? But first a little cover-up . . ."

I would very much have liked the pavement to open up and swallow me whole right then. As if it wasn't bad enough to have someone dabbing at the crater on my face with a makeup sponge, there Daniel was, doing it right in front of a sidewalk full of spectators. And Mateo. I wanted to die.

Just in case I wasn't already squirming from embarrassment, he asked, "Do you think we could lose the retainer? We don't want the cameras to pick up any glare off the wire."

It wasn't a retainer; it was a palate expander, but I wasn't going to argue details. "Um, the case is up in my room," I said, pointing back to the building.

"No time," Daniel declared, as if I'd asked permission to go back and get it. He held out a baggie and a small paper napkin. "Go ahead and put it in there. It will be safe in the box."

Okay, have you ever taken one of those things out of your mouth? You know how the spit kind of dribbles and stretches and . . . I so did not want to deal with all that in front of an audience. I was completely mortified, but when I glanced up, Mateo was tactfully looking the other way.

I pulled the expander out of my mouth as quickly as I could and wrapped it in the napkin, stringy spit and all. Once it was safely sealed in the plastic bag, I handed it to Daniel. He tucked the bag into one of the many compartments in his makeup box, brushed a little clear gloss on my lips, and announced that I was done.

I decided if I could live through the humiliation of the makeup chair, I could handle anything else the day had in store for me.

I am so very naive.

The whole premise of my mom and dad's show is that we're supposed to learn about an area by living like the locals. That's how they came up with the name. You know: "When in Rome, do as the Romans do." But I have to tell you, it's pretty hard to do as the Romans do—or in this case, the Valencians—when there's a camera in your face.

It must have taken us twenty minutes to walk from the Plaza de la Reina, where we were staying, to the Plaza del Ayuntamiento, where we were supposed to catch the bus. It probably should have taken only five. Filming is bad enough on a regular day, but Daniel was taking his temporary cameraman job way too seriously.

"Look this way." "Turn that way." "Head up." "Chin down." "Walk more naturally." "Cassidy, you need to be more social, sweetheart."

More social? Was he kidding? He was choreographing every step.

Whenever I felt like saying something back to him, I'd catch my mom watching me, and I'd paste the smile back on my face and toss my hair or whatever other inane thing Daniel kept shouting at me to do.

When we finally reached the Plaza del Ayuntamiento, Daniel declared he was parched and told us all to take five while he hurried off with Bayani to find some bottled water to take with us.

The plaza was like a lot of the huge market squares I've seen in other European cities. Basically, it was just a stone courtyard lined with trees. Along one side was a row of flower booths and at the narrow end, separated by a busy road, was a fountain.

Mateo pointed out a round building down the street. "There is the Plaza de Toros," he said. "The bullfighting ring."

I elbowed Victoria. "Ooh. Maybe we should go there so you can meet some handsome matadors."

She smiled but shook her head. "I'm afraid matadors and I would not get along."

I just about opened my big mouth to agree with her. From our Spanish culture study, I knew Victoria thought bullfighting was inhumane and cruel. It wasn't something I'd ever want to see in real life, either. I mean, if it was just the matador waving his cape at the bull, sure. But as soon as the picadors start poking the poor animal with their spears, no thank you. Still, bullfighting was part of Mateo's culture, and I didn't want to hurt his feelings by saying anything rude about it.

So I changed the subject.

"It's really bright out here." I shaded my eyes and squinted at Victoria. "Can we go look at the vendor carts? Maybe I can find some sunglasses. I forgot mine."

"You and Mateo go ahead," she said. "I . . . need to make a call." She pointed to the phone in her hand. Smooth. Could she have been any less subtle about pushing Mateo and me together?

I quickly turned away from him to scan the plaza so he couldn't see the blush I could feel creeping up my cheeks. "Where's a good place to start?" I asked. "He's got glasses over there." I pointed to a guy with a blanket spread on the ground in front of him. On the blanket, all kinds of sunglasses were lined up in neat rows. Here and there throughout the open space other vendors without booths were selling stuff from blankets on the ground as well.

"Those are called top *manta*," Mateo said.

"*Manta*," I repeated. "That means blanket, right?"

Mateo nodded. "They don't have a license to sell, so they lay out what they can on top of the blanket. If the authorities come looking, they will quickly grab the blanket with all their things and run away."

"Oh. They have the same kind of vendors in New York City. They sell the knockoff designer stuff, right?" Actually, it seemed to be a universal thing. I'd seen the same kind of thing in Hong Kong, and London, and Paris, and about any other large city we'd been to.

"Let's see what they have in the booths."

We wandered up and down the row of stalls, stopping here and there to try on sunglasses and hats. I couldn't help stealing glances at Mateo. Like I said, I didn't have much experience with guys, so spending the day with him was surreal. How hard would it be to sneak a picture of him, I wondered. I could always tell him it was for my blog. That wouldn't be a lie. I did need to get more pictures to post and—

"You like? You buy."

My thought bubble disappeared in a poof, and I blinked, confused. "What?"

The man behind the sales table pointed to the sunglasses I had been trying on. "The glasses. You like? You buy."

"Oh. Right." I dug into my purse and handed him a ten-euro coin. He grunted and dropped it with a clank into his till.

I turned to Mateo, daring to full-on stare at him now that my eyes were hidden behind the dark lenses. He stared right back, smiling his brilliant smile, which for some reason made it hard for me to breathe.

But then he kept watching me.

"What?" I demanded.

"They look good," he said.

I practically skipped to the next booth.

We probably wandered to about ten more booths. I found a charm for my necklace—a Moorish cross with a deep red stone in the center of it—and a large fringed scarf with a bright abstract print. It looked like something my gramma would like. I'm thoughtful that way.

Okay, maybe I was feeling a little guilty about how I said I didn't want to go live with her. Or how I really *didn't* want to go live with her. What if she wanted to talk about Grampa being gone? I couldn't handle that. So I bought the scarf for her—but it didn't make me feel better.

It was then that Bayani called everyone together and announced it was time to resume filming. Daniel huffed when he saw me and ordered me to sit for makeup once again because I was getting "shiny." Thank you, Daniel.

He was pretty much a diva like that the rest of the afternoon. I swear, he must have thought we were filming an art house documentary instead of a television show the way he went on about aesthetics and composition.

"I'm sorry," I told Mateo. "He's not usually like this. I think the power is going to his head."

"I don't mind."

But I did. I had to keep reminding myself to be useful whenever Daniel would direct Mateo to stand closer to me or for me to walk a little taller. (What did he want me to do? Balance on my tiptoes?) I kept waiting for Mom or Dad to say something, but Mom was already prepping for her segment, and Dad was too busy strolling down memory lane with Señor Ruiz-Moreno to notice. And laughing like a juvenile.

Which was plain weird. I mean, I know my dad had a life before he turned old and everything, but it was really strange to *see* it.

"Can you just imagine them with long hair and faded jeans, thumbing for rides?" I asked Mateo.

He regarded them for a moment and shuddered. "I don't like to think about it."

"There!" cried Daniel. "The way you just bent your heads together! Do it again!"

I slid a look at Mateo. "I'll hit him high, you hit him low. He'll never see it coming."

But Mateo just laughed.

● ● ● ● ●

The last stop of the morning was the playground at the Turia Park. Okay, so you know in malls and places where they have play areas for kids with really huge flowers or ice cream cones or breakfast foods to play on? Well, this park was kind of like that, only the play structure was a huge Gulliver lying on the ground like he'd just been tied down by Lilliputians.

The entire playground was a football-field-sized Gulliver, all tied up. I am not even kidding.

Daniel hefted his camera and pointed to Mateo and me. "Now climb on up there and slide down his coat," he instructed.

"What, us?" I asked. "Wouldn't it be more authentic to get some shots of *kids* playing on it?"

"You *are* kids," Daniel said matter-of-factly.

"Yeah, but . . ."

I noticed Mom glance up from her notes, watching me again. *Useful*, I told myself. *Useful, useful, useful.* But a playground? What was I, five?

Then Mateo bumped my shoulder with his. "I will if you will."

It was probably his smile that did it. Or the challenge in his voice. Did I mention I like a challenge? Whatever it was, I raced Mateo up the stairs that ran the length of Gulliver's leg and threw myself onto the coat slide. I was even able to ignore Daniel, who was standing at the base of the coat shouting, "Yes! Very good! Now give us a smile! Once more from another angle!"

Up and down, over the hand, the foot, the sword. And then we were supposed to slide down Gulliver's strands of hair. Which would have been okay, except the strand I chose had a small crack in it. Just enough of a crack to snag on the pocket of my shorts. I heard the rip before the sting on my skin registered.

Victoria must have realized something was wrong because she called out, "I believe we have enough for now," and made Daniel put the camera away.

Mateo offered to help me up since I was still sitting on the end of Gulliver's hair, but there's no way I was going to stand until I knew how big the tear was. And where.

"Um, thanks. I'm just . . . going to catch my breath for a minute first, okay?"

He looked at me strangely, but at least he didn't press it.

"Mateo," Victoria said, "why don't you go see if your father is ready to go?" She pointed over to where my dad and Señor Ruiz-Moreno were playing air guitar by Gulliver's foot. Now that Daniel had put his camera away, it's like they thought they had free reign to act like complete idiots. If I hadn't already been thoroughly humiliated, that would have put me over the edge.

"Where is it, then?" Victoria asked once Mateo walked over to his dad.

I stood and turned my back to her.

She started to laugh but caught herself. "Oh, sorry," she said, but she couldn't hide the smile.

"Ha, ha." I reached back to feel the tear in the seat of my shorts and was mortified to touch skin. "What do I *do*?"

"I could take you back to the flat to change," she suggested.

I sat back down. "Only one problem. My suitcase hasn't come yet. I have only one pair of pants besides these, and they're wet. I washed them out this morning."

"I see." She sat next to me and balled her fist under her chin. "I suppose you're stuck, then."

I shot her a look. "I hate it when you do that."

She blinked at me innocently. "Do what?"

"Act like you don't know what to do so I have to come up with the solution."

"I have no idea what you're talking about."

"Right." I folded my arms and looked away. Mateo was over talking to Bayani, but he was looking at me, which made me even more determined to get off the slide.

"Do you have that scarf I gave you to hold?" I asked Victoria.

"Right here," she said, patting her purse.

"Can you help me for a minute?"

We ducked behind Gulliver's head, and Victoria quickly unfolded the scarf. I grabbed it and wrapped it around my hips, tying it on one side like a sarong.

"Turn around," she directed. I did a slow pirouette, and

she watched with a critical eye, tugging here and tucking there. "That looks fine," she said.

I glanced down at my scarf skirt. I'm not sure how fine it looked, but at least the rip was covered.

When we started back toward the group, Daniel spotted Victoria and me right away. "Ooh, I like the change," he called. "*Darling* skirt." He started to lift his camera, but Bayani shook his head.

"We have only fifteen minutes to make it to the *horchateria*," he said. "We've got to wrap it up."

My mom's segment was scheduled to be filmed at the Horchateria de Santa Catalina, which was located back at the Plaza de la Reina, right across from the Santa Catalina chapel. A *horchateria* is a café where they serve a traditional iced drink called *horchata,* which is what my mom's segment was going to be about.

Half the crew members rushed ahead of us to set up security and cameras at the *horchateria.* By the time the rest of us got there, Bayani and the other crew members had already set up rope barricades and a crowd had begun to gather. The crew ushered us inside the roped-off area and stood around us like Secret Service to keep the spectators from getting too close.

"Nice pick, Bayani," my dad said. "This place has character."

"It is one of the most famous *horchaterias* in the area," Señor Ruiz-Moreno agreed. He pointed to the sign over the entrance that read CASA CON DOS SIGLOS DE TRADICIÓN. "Two hundred years of tradition," he translated.

"That's why I chose it," Bayani said proudly.

"My mom always decides on the food segments she wants to do when we're on location," I explained to Mateo, "but Bayani has to set them up and find a venue."

"How do you know where to look?" Mateo asked.

Bayani tapped a finger to his forehead. "Smarts," he said. "Plus I research the history of an area and look for a location with the most character for filming. Take this place, for instance . . ."

Bayani kept talking, and Mateo nodded enough to make it look like he was paying attention; but the way his eyes shifted this way and that, it was obvious he was getting distracted by the growing crowd. I guess Bayani picked up on it, too, because he let his story taper off, and he turned to talk to Dad and Señor Ruiz-Moreno instead. Mateo didn't even seem to notice.

"How do you get used to this?" he asked me in a low voice.

"Bayani's not that bad," I said. "Kind of annoying sometimes, but—"

"No," Mateo said. "Not Bayani. Them." He gave a little nod toward the people pushing up against our sound technician's back, trying to get a better view. "Isn't it weird to have people watching you all day?"

"You get used to it." I shrugged like having a following was old news. I didn't remind him that I was usually in the background helping the crew, and that most people are interested in gawking only at the ones who are in front of the cameras. This was the first time the crowd was actually paying attention to *me*. And seriously? I thought it was kind of fun swishing my hair and hiding behind my dark glasses, pretending to be a celebrity. I noticed a couple of ladies near the front of the crowd taking pictures with their cell-phone cameras, and I nudged Mateo. We fake-posed, pouted, and puckered until they turned their phones on someone else.

"What are we waiting for?" I asked my dad. I plucked at my damp shirt. "It's hot out here."

"Daniel wants shots of you entering the establishment," Bayani said. "He has to get the equipment set up."

I didn't care about equipment at that point. All I knew was that inside the *horchateria* were air-conditioning, chairs to sit on, and something cold to drink. Outside on the sidewalk, sweat was prickling down my back. I'm sure my face was getting shiny again. And, despite what I had told Mateo, I didn't like people staring at me like a bug under a microscope.

Finally, with Daniel's approval, we were allowed to enter the *horchateria*. The cool air raised goose bumps on my damp skin, and I closed my eyes, breathing a sigh of relief.

"No, no, no. Again, please, without the theatrics this time." Daniel shooed us back out the door. I wanted to strangle him, but Mateo chuckled beside me.

"Be serious," Mateo warned as we walked inside again. Both of us scowled and stalked toward a table.

"Again!" Daniel cried.

He made us walk through the door three times. We probably would have kept tormenting him so he'd never get his shot, but my mom gave me a pointed look from the corner of the shop where she had set up for her segment.

Useful, I reminded myself, and allowed Daniel to direct us. Fortunately, he had to go film the foodie segment next, so we would be free of him for a while.

A waitress in a black uniform showed us to a table where we could drink our *horchatas* while we watched my mom do her segment.

The *horchateria* looked kind of like an old-fashioned ice cream parlor back in the States, only fancier. It had a colorful mural on the wall, a black-and-white tiled floor, and long glass counters filled with sugared pastries that looked kind of like those you can buy at an American carnival. Our table even had a round marble top. Señor Ruiz-Moreno ordered for us, and the waitress hurried off.

"Have you ever had *horchata* before, *niña*?" he asked.

"Only the Mexican kind," I told him.

"Our *horchata de chufa* is better," Mateo assured me.

"That she can decide for herself," Señor Ruiz-Moreno said, winking. And then to me he added, "Mexican *horchata* is made from rice, but the Valencian *horchata* is made from *chufa*. How do you call it? Tiger nuts. They are grown right here in this region."

The drink came, and I took a long sip. It had been a long time since I'd had rice *horchata,* so I didn't remember it enough to describe the difference; but this was milky, sweet, and cold, and that's all that mattered. Along with the *horchata,* the waitress had also brought a plate of pastries from the glass counter.

"Dunk one," Mateo said. "It's very good."

I picked up a pastry and dipped it into my glass. "Like this?"

"Yeah. Now—"

"Shh!" Daniel hissed. "We're filming."

We ate and drank quietly while my mom smiled into the camera and talked about the *chufa* plant like it was the most interesting thing in the world. She explained how *chufa* had been brought to Spain from Egypt. The Moors had cultivated it into an important crop in the Valencian region.

Next, some guy from the shop joined her to show how *horchata de chufa* was made.

I'd already heard all about it back at our apartment while she was preparing for the shoot, so I started to zone out. I counted the tiles behind her head and then followed the checkerboard pattern around the wall to the front door. Outside, the barricades had been taken down. Several gawkers had pressed forward and now watched us through the glass like we were a living exhibit at a museum or something. I didn't like that image, so I turned it around so that they were the ones on display.

Just then my phone began to buzz and vibrate, and I slapped my hand over my pocket to muffle the sound. It was 4:35, the time I had set my alarm for that morning. I must have switched it from A.M. to P.M. instead of turning it off. And now it was in my shorts pocket, under the scarf skirt. Great.

Daniel turned from the camera long enough to shoot an icy glare in my direction. I had to untie the scarf to pull my phone out of my pocket and turn it off.

"Brava," Mateo whispered. He looked like he was trying to hold back the laughter, but I wasn't sure if it was because of my alarm or my scarf. Or both.

I ignored him (and the burning in my cheeks). Setting the phone on the table, I turned my attention to retying the knot in the scarf. It might look a little off when I stood up, but at least the air-conditioning in my shorts would be covered.

"There," Mateo said.

I looked up to see that he was holding my phone.

"I entered my number in your contacts," he said, handing it back to me. "Now you have to text me so I can have yours."

"Oh," I said. I'm articulate like that. The only people I ever texted were my mom and dad and Victoria. Sometimes Bayani. But that was way different than texting a boy socially. This was a big moment for me.

I cradled the phone. It was still warm from his hands. (All right. I know it was probably warm from riding around in my pocket all day, but he *had* just been holding it, and that's what counts.)

Just as I was about to type in a text to Mateo, Bayani called out, "Okay, everyone. That's a wrap. Go unwind, and we'll meet up again in front of the apartment building at five thirty sharp."

My dad stood up, his chair scraping over the tile floor. "You coming, Cassie-bug?"

I winced. "Dad!"

He chuckled and patted me on the shoulder. "You know, when you were a little girl—"

I cut him off before he could humiliate me any further. "Go on. I'll be right there." I turned back to the phone and quickly sent my number to Mateo's.

"People!" Bayani shouted. "If you're not clearing out, you're packing up!"

"Wow," I told him. "You sound really authoritative."

"You mean bossy."

"That, too."

Mateo stayed with me, and we helped Bayani finish cleaning up the shoot. By the time we walked back outside into the heat, the crowds had disappeared. And so had the rest of the crew. Bayani shifted the box of cables, extension cords, and gaffer tape he was carrying and looked down the street to where everyone else was clustered in front of our apartment building, talking and laughing. We trudged down the hot sidewalk to join them.

"Cavin better be here before we leave for Buñol tonight," he grumbled. "I don't want his job anymore."

"If he gets here, does that mean you can take over for Daniel?" I asked. "Please?"

Bayani laughed. "What? I thought Daniel was your friend."

"Well, yeah. But I think this film thing has gone to his head."

"People!" Mateo mimicked. "Once more with feeling!"

With his Spanish accent, Mateo sounded even more dramatic than Daniel himself. I had to laugh.

"No theatrics!" Mateo warned.

"Good!" Bayani said. "There he is."

I thought he meant Daniel and I winced, hoping Daniel hadn't heard us. Just because he'd been making me crazy all day didn't mean I wanted to hurt his feelings. But then I realized who Bayani was waving to. It was Cavin, just climbing out of a taxicab. "Come on," I said to Mateo, "you've got to meet him."

"But wait!" Mateo held back, holding his hands up to form a frame. "I must capture the moment."

"No, really," I said, pulling on his arm. "You're going to like—" And then I stumbled to a stop right in front of the cab and stared.

Because standing behind Cavin was a tall, dark-haired boy with laughing green eyes I would know anywhere. He cocked his head to the side and looked straight at me.

"Hello, Cassidy," he said.

7

Logan McCarthy and I practically grew up together. Okay, we were together for only three years—from the time I was seven and he was eight until I was almost ten and he was eleven—but those were crucial years as far as I was concerned. Logan's dad was with *When in Rome* way back when it started, and in those days Logan, like me, had traveled from location to location with the show. Then, two years ago, his mom decided he'd had enough "ladding about," and she'd taken him back to Ireland to live with her.

I cried for days after he left. He and I used to do everything together, and I missed him terribly—even though he always managed to get me into trouble. He'd dare me to do crazy things, and I could never resist the challenge. I'd have to do whatever he said so he wouldn't think I was a baby. Then he'd do something even crazier to show me up, and it kept going from there. He was my best friend. And then one day he was gone.

He never said good-bye when he left. Never wrote, never called. Sometimes I'd see Ireland listed among the visitor stats on my blog, and I wanted to think it was him, but I never knew for sure.

I made lists and lists of all the things I would tell Logan if I ever saw him again, but now that he was standing right in front of me, I couldn't think of a single word to say. I mean, a lot had changed since he left. I had changed. And, by the look of him, so had he.

This Logan still had the same easy grin as the boy I once knew, and the same mischievous glint in his eyes, but his dark hair was longer—just brushing the top of his collar now—and his face had become more angular. Sharper somehow, like it was just coming into focus. So, he was still my Logan, but he was also a stranger.

How was I supposed to greet an ex-friend/stranger? Hug? Handshake? Punch in the face? While I stood there like an idiot trying to figure it out, Bayani pushed past me and gave Logan one of those chest-bump, slap-on-the-back kind of guy hugs. "Hey, man. Welcome back. Good to see you again!"

"Thanks, Yans," Logan said, using his old nickname for Bayani. He slapped Bayani's back in return, and then, when they were done male bonding, he reached out a hand to Victoria. "Miss Chen. How have you been?"

Victoria pressed her lips together to hide a smile as she shook his hand. "My. So formal, Logan."

It's Da's fault." He grinned and shrugged one shoulder. "He said I had to 'behave myself.'"

"And don't you forget it, boyo," Cavin said, smacking Logan on the back of the head.

By the time I had recovered enough to say anything, my moment to greet Logan smoothly was gone. Dad had already started introducing Logan and Cavin to Mateo and Señor Ruiz-Moreno.

"Futbol fan?" Mateo pointed to the logo on Logan's shirt. It showed a green soccer ball with the words FAI IRE-LAND above it.

"Always," Logan said.

Mateo's eyes lit up. "You know Los Che?"

"Of course. I watch La Liga."

I just stood there feeling stupider by the second. It's like they were speaking a foreign language. (Okay, so they *were* speaking a foreign language. Plus neither one of them even seemed to remember I was still there.) Leave it to Logan to spoil everything. Mateo was *my* . . . playdate. Or at least he had been before Logan came along and Mateo forgot all about me. I gave up and left them to go over to stand with my dad.

He and Cavin were skimming over the itinerary Bayani had prepared. "The train ride to Buñol takes around forty-five minutes, so that should give everyone time to get settled in before we need to set up for the cook-off segment." He glanced at Cavin. "You going to be up for that?"

"Sure, and why not?" Cavin answered, patting his stomach. "Food trumps sleep every time." He chuckled at his own joke and then turned to Logan. "Right, son. Come get the bags."

Logan tucked his duffel under one arm and hefted a suitcase in each hand. I was about to offer to get the other bags for him, but Mateo beat me to it and grabbed everything that was left.

They don't need me, I thought sourly as they carried the bags to the front door. I hated feeling like an outsider. Even more, I hated not being able to define the bitterness I felt as I watched them go. I couldn't decide if I was angrier at Logan for stealing Mateo, or at Mateo for abandoning me, or at both of them for leaving me out. All I knew was that Logan had been in Valencia only ten minutes, and Mateo had already forgotten I was alive.

"You're not concentrating," Victoria said when I gave the wrong definition for our third vocabulary word in a row.

I sighed and slumped over the table. Because of the festival the next day, we wouldn't be having lessons, so Victoria had decided to cram homework into every free minute before we left for Buñol. Which meant while everyone else had free time before going to the train, I was stuck doing stupid vocabulary.

Not only that, but I couldn't stop running the day with Mateo through my head again and again, reliving every laugh and smile, right up to the point when Logan took him away. It didn't matter how many times I played it back, the end result was always the same. I hated the way it made me feel—angry and sad and happy and hopeful all mixed up together so that none of it made sense.

Victoria closed her book. "What is it?" she asked. "We may as well talk about it, or we'll never get anything done."

Even if I had wanted to spill my guts to Victoria, I wouldn't have known where to begin to talk about it. Everything I was feeling was foreign and new. So I just settled for a simple question. "How do you know if you really like somebody?"

"Oh," she said. "I see. Well, I think it might be different for everyone, but for me, I feel a kind of zing when I'm with someone I truly care for. It's like an electric current—quick and tingly and thrilling. Any particular reason you're asking?"

"Just curious," I said, suddenly very interested in the worksheet in front of me.

Victoria watched quietly for a moment and then mused, "What a pleasant surprise to have Logan back with the show."

I glanced up. "Yeah, I guess."

"What's he been doing the last couple of years, I wonder?"

"I wouldn't know," I grumbled.

"Ah."

That's all she said. Just 'ah.' But it sounded like it meant a whole lot more. And that made me defensive. I felt like I had to explain why I was upset, even though I didn't understand it myself.

"He never wrote," I said.

"Did you write to him?"

"I e-mailed a couple times. Sent some letters with Cavin. But Logan never wrote back. When he left, he was just gone."

She nodded and started fitting her books into her bag. "Did I ever tell you about my friend Sylvie?" she asked. "She lives in Barcelona. When we were in school, we were the best of friends. We did everything together."

Like Logan and me, I thought. Subtle.

"When we graduated," she continued, "I began traveling and teaching, and Sylvie moved to Spain. We're still very good friends, and I stop in to visit her whenever I'm in Barcelona, but we seldom make contact in between."

"Will you see her this trip?" I asked.

"Yes, as a matter of fact, I'll go to visit her after we return from La Tomatina. But the point is that a friendship is a valuable thing. Too valuable to give up just because you don't have a tether to each other when you're apart. A true friendship is one you can pick up where you left off and move forward without looking back."

That sounded all fine and wonderful and everything, but I bet Sylvie wasn't elbowing in on Victoria's cute new Spanish friend. I didn't want to talk about it anymore.

"You should probably rest now," Victoria said. "The cook-off doesn't start until late this evening, and I understand you were up quite early this morning."

"Oh, my gosh." I threw up my hands. "Is there any detail of my life that everyone doesn't know?"

"Of course not." She stood and settled the strap of her bag over her shoulder. "See you tonight, Cassidy."

Travel tip: In Spain, appearance is very important. A foreigner who wishes to make a good impression will try to show good taste in dress.

The airline called. They said they'd found our bags, but they wouldn't be able to deliver them until after the time we had to leave to catch our train. Dad made arrangements for the luggage to be sent straight to Buñol, but the airline couldn't guarantee what time they'd get it there.

When he told me the news, I slogged to my room and dropped onto the desk chair. The universe sure had a stupid sense of humor. I finally meet a guy worth crushing on and make my big debut in front of the camera, and I had nothing to wear but my torn shorts and scarf sarong.

It's the kind of thing Logan and I might have laughed about once upon a time. But I didn't want to think about Logan. I didn't want to dwell on my missing clothes. Neither one was going to do me any good.

At least I could update my blog without worrying about what not to wear. Or about old friends dropping in. Or new friends dropping out. I pulled out my laptop and booted it up. There wasn't much time left before we had to leave for the train, but if I hurried, I could get a quick entry posted with the video from that morning.

I copied the images from my phone to my computer and flipped through them on the screen. The last picture to come up was the one I had snapped of Mateo in the market plaza. A warm tingle rolled over me when I saw him smiling out at me from the computer screen. Not quite the zing Victoria described, but it was definitely something.

A knock on the door startled me out of la-la land, and I jumped to switch screens just before the door opened.

My mom poked her head into the room. "Five minutes, Cassidy."

She made me promise I'd be ready to go, as if I had

anything to do to *get* ready. It's not like I had a suitcase
to pack. I did want to get the blog post done though, so I
started the video uploading while I zipped up my backpack
to take on the trip.

It took so long for the video to finish uploading, I didn't
have time to do much editing once it did. If I was lucky, I'd
barely be able to smooth out that spot where I'd had to grab
my phone before it dropped into the—

Aw, man! I leaned closer to the screen. Some idiot had
pulled a delivery van right in front of the Door of the Apostles while I was filming. I mean, you could still see the door
and the cathedral and everything, but a van in the picture
kind of spoiled the medieval mood I *thought* I had captured
on film that morning.

Perfect. I sounded like Daniel. The video would do. I
typed up a quick description of the sights and sounds and
posted the blog and signed off just as Dad knocked on the
door and said it was time to go.

I should have been paying closer attention.

Bayani had tried to reserve a train car for the crew to ride together, but of course the day before the Tomatina Festival was not a good time to try to hog seats between Valencia and Buñol. It's also not a good time to haul suitcases and equipment onto the train. Señor Ruiz-Moreno volunteered to drive and take everyone's stuff to Buñol, which was cool and everything except for the fact that he took Mateo with him.

"Don't worry," Bayani teased. "You'll get to see him there."

"Shut up," I said. I'm known for my great comebacks.

The train was packed. We were lucky to find enough seats for everyone, let alone sit in the same car. A lot of other people were left standing.

Victoria pointed to where Logan was stuffing his duffel onto the overhead rack. "I'll bet Logan could use a seat-mate."

"I'm pretty sure his dad's sitting with him." I slipped past her to take the empty seat next to where we were standing and scooted over to the window. According to Victoria, I should just be happy Logan was back and forget how he never answered my letters and e-mails for two years. I might have been willing to consider that if he hadn't shown up unannounced with no apology and stole the attention of my possible zing.

"Just as well," she said, taking the seat next to mine. "We can use the time to work on your vocabulary lesson."

Homework was a lost cause. I couldn't concentrate on words when all I could think about was Mateo. And Logan. And Mateo *and* Logan. And me, left out. Between that and the lulling rhythm of the train, there was no way I could focus on the flip cards Victoria was showing me.

It took a while, but she finally gave up. "Perhaps this is not the best idea." She tucked the cards into her bag and stood. "If you'll excuse me, I need to go speak with Cavin for a moment."

"But he's sitting with Logan," I said stupidly.

"Precisely." Victoria left me with a smile.

I let my head fall back against the seat. Great. What was

I supposed to say to Logan? Thanks for ignoring me while you were gone. Oh, yes, and since you got back, too.

I didn't have time to think about it too much, because just then Logan parked himself on the seat beside me.

"Man, it's hot in here." He flapped his shirt. "You hot?"

"Mmmm," I said.

"You remember when we were in Spain last time? Freezing our butts off in Granada?"

"Mmmm."

"Pretty much different this time around."

"Mmmm."

"Da says you're to be in the show."

"Look, Logan. No offense, but I'm really tired." I closed my eyes, hoping he'd get the hint that I didn't want to talk.

It worked for a few minutes. It probably would have worked longer if I'd been able to keep my eyes shut. But if I kept them shut, I couldn't see him, and I wouldn't know if he was watching me or ignoring me or making faces at me or what. So I opened one eye a crack. He was watching me.

"What?" I demanded.

"I knew you weren't asleep."

"You did not."

He just smiled at that. "Just like old times."

I closed my eye again. "Not really."

"How've you been?"

"Phenomenal."

He didn't say anything again for a long while, until finally I couldn't stand it any longer. I opened both eyes. He grinned like he'd just won some supreme challenge. I wanted to hit him.

"What's wrong?" he asked.

Dork. What did he *think* was wrong? If he didn't know, I wasn't going to tell him.

Until he sat there and watched me all quiet again.

"I never heard from you," I said finally.

He nodded slowly like he had to consider my words before answering. "I never heard from you, either."

"Not true. I e-mailed. I wrote letters."

"Never got 'em."

I clenched my jaw and looked away.

"Hey," he said. "I'm sorry."

"Are you?"

"Truly. I didn't mean to make you mad."

"I'm not mad," I snapped.

He coughed to cover his laugh.

I had to admit, it was just like old times. This was our pattern: he'd joke, I'd get mad, he'd laugh, I'd get madder. Mom used to tell me he teased only because he could get a "rise" out of me. The only way to stop it would be not to fall into the trap.

"Okay, so maybe I was a little mad. But I'll get over it. Truce?" I held out my hand, and he shook it.

"Deal." He hesitated for a minute and then added, "I

would'a written you a message, but the comments on your blog were turned off."

"You read my blog?" Maybe those Ireland hits in the stat counter actually *were* him. He hadn't completely forgotten about me.

I almost let myself get misty about it, but then he shrugged like it was no big deal. "I should get back," he said, standing. "Nice talking to you, Cass."

Victoria came back to sit by me just as the scenery outside the train began to scroll past the window slower and slower. Crossing gates *ding, ding, ding*ed as we rolled up to a little station. A red sign at the side of the tracks said BUÑOL.

"Well, here we are," Victoria said. I think she kept talking, but I had tuned her out. Because there, standing on the platform with his dad, was Mateo.

I pressed my hand to the glass. Mateo saw me. He waved, and I went all fizzy inside.

The train hadn't even come to a stop before people started crowding into the aisle. I grabbed my backpack and jumped up to join them, but Victoria didn't move.

"Not so fast," she said. "Daniel said he wanted to get some shots of you and your parents arriving at the station once the train has emptied out a little."

I sighed and sank back down in my seat. Logan gave me a cheerful wave as he and his dad passed by. Minutes later, I saw them outside on the platform, walking over to where

Mateo and his dad were standing. It just figured that Logan would get to Mateo first.

By the time Daniel was ready to film my mom and dad and me waving to the camera, the train was completely empty. Even Victoria had left us to join the rest of the crew. On the platform, Mateo and Logan were already talking and gesturing with their hands, completely oblivious to us. As much as I had wished to be in front of the camera, I wished even more I was over there with them instead of fake-smiling for Daniel.

"Cassidy, darling," Daniel said as he squinted at me through the lens, "I need you to smile. This is supposed to be a happy moment."

I watched Logan air-kick an invisible soccer ball to Mateo, who air–head butted it back to him, and I sighed. *Yeah. Ecstatic.*

Still, I did what I had to do—wave and smile like a homecoming queen, and pantomime how delighted I was by my first sight of Buñol.

Daniel made my mom and dad and me climb off the train at least five times before he was satisfied with the shot. I'd been smiling for so long my cheeks were beginning to hurt. Cavin and Bayani were no help. They chatted on the platform with Señor Ruiz-Moreno, not even paying attention to us. Great directing skills.

Daniel didn't let up until Señor Ruiz-Moreno said it was time we leave for his brother's house. Daniel looked like he was going to follow us there, until Bayani gently suggested they get settled at the hotel before going to set up for the paella cook-off.

"Son," Cavin called to Logan, "it's time we were going, as well."

Suddenly, I found a reason to smile. Cavin and Logan were staying in the hotel with the crew, of course. Only my mom and dad and I would be staying at Mateo's uncle's house. Which meant Logan couldn't monopolize Mateo all afternoon.

Logan said good-bye to Mateo and almost walked right past me on his way over to his dad. Then, like he suddenly remembered I was there, he turned and gave me a chin jerk. "See you tonight."

I balled up my fists and was about to tell him what I thought about his manners, but my mom squeezed my arm as a not-so-subtle reminder that we were always "on." Always.

So I gave him a plastic smile and a princess wave. He didn't even notice.

Now that Logan was gone, Mateo came over to where my mom and dad and I were standing. "I can take your bag," he said.

"It's okay," I said automatically, and then mentally kicked myself. *No, stupid. Let the boy take your bag.* "I mean, um, thanks for offering."

"Well, it is a far way to walk."

"Walk? I thought your dad had a car."

"Yes. But he cannot drive it now that the barricades are set. The roads are closed for the festival, and so we walk."

He didn't wait for me to say no again but took my backpack from me and slung a strap over his shoulder. At least *someone* knew how to be a gentleman.

"*Gracias,*" I said.

He smiled his brilliant smile. *"No pasa nada."*

Señor Ruiz-Moreno's brother's house wasn't really a house. Not in the traditional sense, anyway. His family lived in a narrow building above their electronics shop. A large sitting room and kitchen occupied the floor directly above the shop. On the floors above that were several bedrooms and bathrooms.

"You're certain they don't mind our staying here," my mom asked for about the tenth time as we stood outside the shop, waiting as Señor Ruiz-Moreno rang the bell.

He laughed. "My brother was happy for a reason to stay in town for La Tomatina this year. His wife usually arranges a vacation in August to escape. She has taken my wife this time and left him with us."

"Doesn't she like the festival?" I asked.

"The festival, perhaps," he said. "The crowds and the mess, definitely not."

I glanced around the quiet street. "It doesn't seem that crowded."

Mateo laughed. "Just wait." He pointed down the narrow street. "The trucks roll right through here. There will be so many people, one can hardly move."

Just then the door opened, and a tall man with salt-and-pepper hair burst out, taking Señor Ruiz-Moreno in a bear hug. "Hector," he said in a booming voice. "*¿Que hay?*"

He barely released Señor Ruiz-Moreno when he turned to Mateo. "*¡Muchacho!*"

"*Tío.*" Mateo stepped forward and was swallowed in his uncle's arms.

"Alberto," Señor Ruiz-Moreno cut in, "allow me to introduce my good friend Davidson Barnett."

Tío Alberto set Mateo down and stretched out a huge hand to my dad. "Of course," he said, pumping my dad's hand up and down. "I have seen you on the television. And this"—he looked to my mom—"is your beautiful wife."

Mom smiled as he took her hand in both of his, and I swear her cheeks turned a darker pink.

"*Encantado,*" Tío Alberto said. "I am enchanted."

"May I present my daughter, Cassidy," Mom said.

"Pleased to meet you, Cassidy." He stood to the side of the door. "Please come in. *Mi casa es su casa.*"

From the front door, a narrow staircase stretched up to the living quarters. The first level was small, but very cozy, with a kitchen in the back and a nice, comfy couch tucked into the front room.

• • • •

Travel tip: The Spanish love to converse and can talk for hours. In fact, they even have a tradition for getting together to talk, called a *tertulia*.

I made the mistake of sinking onto the oversized cushions on the couch as soon as Tío Alberto had given us a quick tour of the house. I couldn't help it. Both Señor Ruiz-Moreno and his brother were talking so much and so fast it made my head spin. After a while, the voices started to blend together until the whole conversation turned into white noise. Somewhere in my head, I knew it was rude not to be attentive to our host, but I couldn't work up the energy to worry about it at that point.

Mateo sat down beside me. I didn't remember his entering the room. I didn't remember much of anything.

"You look tired." His voice sounded far away.

It took a whole lot more effort to look over at him than it should have. I think I said something to him, but I can't be sure. The last thing I remembered was his smile and the warm, irresistible pull of sleep.

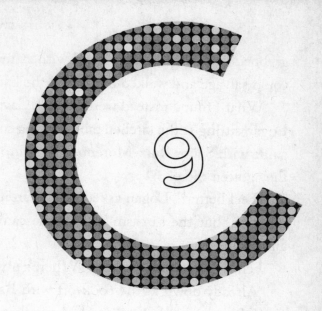

"Cassidy."

Someone tugged at my arm. I tried to turn away, but something was blocking me.

My eyes snapped open.

Mateo. My head was resting on his shoulder.

I bolted upright.

"Hey, Sleeping Beauty," my dad said.

I groaned and shot him a look. *Really, Dad? It's not enough that I fell asleep on a guy I've known for only one afternoon? You need to compound the embarrassment?*

But Dad was oblivious, as usual. "It's about time," he said. "You want to freshen up?"

Beside me, Mateo began to silently chuckle. *Perfect.* I

grabbed my backpack and stood with as much dignity as I could salvage and walked off to find the bathroom.

What I found instead were Daniel, Cavin, Victoria, and Logan sitting at the kitchen table playing some kind of card game with Señor Ruiz-Moreno and his brother. When had they gotten there?

"Feel better?" Logan asked. It was an innocent enough question, but the sarcasm in his tone came through loud and clear.

I chose not to answer him. "Where's my mom?" I asked.

"Already down at the cook-off with Bayani," Dad said from the doorway behind me. "It's nearly nine o'clock."

I glanced out the window, where the sky was painted rose and purple. My head said it was sunset, but my body felt like it should be sunrise. I yawned.

"No more of that," Daniel scolded. "We need you to look alive tonight."

"Me? My mom's the one doing the cook-off. And if Bayani's already there with her—"

"I've asked Daniel to man a second camera," Cavin said. "He can get some candid shots of the rest of the group while Bayani and the crew work the festival."

Perfect. Daniel still behind the camera. Just my luck.

He fluttered his hands. "Now run along and get ready. Time waits for no one, least of all sleepy TV stars."

● ● ● ● ●

I escaped to the bathroom and pressed a cold washrag to my face. My hair was all flat on one side where I had been leaning (and thankfully not drooling) on Mateo's shoulder. I brushed it back as well as I could and pulled it into a low ponytail. By now, my scarf skirt was pretty wrinkled, but without my suitcase, I didn't have a whole lot of wardrobe options. I untied the scarf and hung it over the towel rack, running the washcloth over the worst of the wrinkles. The rest I smoothed down with my hand. That would have to be good enough. At least it was getting dark soon. And maybe Daniel could just film me from the waist up.

Still, as I checked myself in the mirror, I had to admit that, wrinkles aside, the scarf didn't really look that bad. The hair was okay, too, I decided. And the sunburn blush from walking around Valencia all day made my eyes look bluer. Adding a little lip gloss, I decided I might actually look presentable, if not kind of, well . . . nice.

By the time I made it back to the kitchen, everyone had already started filing down the narrow front steps. Logan had snagged Mateo, of course. They stood at the top of the stairs, talking. Mateo glanced back toward me for an instant, but then Logan said something and his attention snapped right back to him. My confidence took a hit.

Then, to make things worse, Daniel took one look at me and grimaced. He *tsk*ed and scurried back to where I stood. "Here, sweetheart. Let me help you with this." Before

I could stop him, he adjusted the scarf around my hips, messing with the knot until it hung perfectly at the side. He pulled the ribbon from my hair next, dropping it onto the kitchen table.

"Now flip your hair forward," he told me. When I hesitated, he grabbed my shoulders and bent me over double, quickly combing his fingers through my hair. "Now flip it back."

This time I did the flipping on my own. My hair settled around my shoulders, and Daniel smoothed a couple of strands, nodding his approval.

"Much better," he proclaimed. "Remember, natural is your friend. Now come on."

I was relieved to see that Mateo and Logan hadn't hung around to witness the impromptu primping. On the other hand, I was a little disappointed that they hadn't waited for me, either.

Everyone had gathered in the street in front of the electronics shop. Well, everyone except Mateo and Logan. They were too busy arguing over who was the better striker on Manchester United. Then they found a stone on the cobbled street and started kicking it back and forth to each other.

I didn't realize I was scowling at them until Daniel nudged me and reminded me that a smile would be much more attractive. Then he hoisted his camera and called to everyone to just act natural.

Of course, it would have been easier to act natural without the camera in my face. Or without the audience that was beginning to gather along the street. Or without having to pretend I was happy when I really was not.

Cavin pulled my dad, Señor Ruiz-Moreno, and Tío Alberto aside to give them instructions on the shots and conversation they wanted to get on film.

"Alberto," he said, "you talk a little about the history of the tomato festival. When did La Tomatina start, what's it like for the locals, et cetera, et cetera. Davidson, you flesh out the cultural details as the three of you stroll along together. Got it? Good."

Victoria came and stood next to me. "You look charming," she said.

I must have still been tired because having her tell me that made my throat go tight. The way Mateo and Logan were ignoring me was beginning to make me feel invisible. "Thanks."

"Very nice." Daniel trained his camera on us. "Like sisters. Now let's see more of the same as we walk to the—"

Victoria held her hand in front of her face. "Turn it off."

"You look beautiful."

"Daniel," she warned. "You know I don't like to be filmed."

He lowered the camera for a moment, looking unsure for the first time that day. Then he straightened, like he remembered the importance of his job. "Then get out of the shot."

She rolled her eyes at him and pulled away from me.

"You want me out of the shot, too?" I asked innocently.

"Ha, ha," Daniel said. "Everyone's a comedian. Now let's get down to that cook-off before the paella gets cold." He glanced up from the viewfinder. "Here we go. We're walking, we're walking . . . Cassidy, head up, sweetheart. That's it."

Daniel micromanaged me all the way to the plaza where the cook-off was being held. Do this, do that. Faster, slower. Meanwhile, Mateo and Logan shouted and laughed behind us, and that made me increasingly angry. Not for any real reason I can name . . . except it didn't seem fair. Okay, fine. It was *my* mom and dad's show we were filming. But still. How come I had to play to the camera and they could just do whatever they wanted?

Without me.

Travel tip: The people of Spain love festivities and any kind of celebrations.

Even my bad mood was no match for the party atmosphere of the cook-off. The entire plaza was crammed with laughing, drinking, happy people. Toward what I assumed was the front of the plaza, long, paper-covered tables groaned under the weight of countless huge iron pans of paella.

If you've never had paella, it's a rice dish that's cooked over an open flame in a big round shallow pan. Supposedly, paella originated in the Valencia region of Spain, which is why it's such a big deal there. Each region and/or chef has his own way of preparing paella, so you could end up getting shrimp, fish, rabbit, chicken, tomatoes, onions, or just about anything in the rice. Even snails. I've had really good paella and I've had really bad paella, and I wasn't sure I was up for taking a chance on sampling too much.

One of the festival coordinators showed us to a table that had been saved for our group. It was roped off from the others right up front in what I guess was supposed to be a place of honor, but it just looked lonely. At least we had the best view from there of where my mom was standing with the paella that she and the local guy had made. Bayani and Daniel filmed her from different angles as she stirred and smiled, stirred and smiled.

We sat on some really uncomfortable folding chairs, Mateo on one side of me and Logan on the other.

Mateo leaned close and whispered, "This is the first time I've sat at the celebrity table."

"Don't let it go to your head," I whispered back.

"Shhh!" Daniel hissed. "The judging is about to begin!"

I won't bore you with the results. Let's just say that with so many entrants, it took a long, long time. My mom didn't win, but she'd be the first to tell you that winning wasn't the point. She had learned to make paella from someone who had a history with it, and that's all that mattered.

See, my mom has a theory. She says a country's story is told through the things its people eat. Food, she says, is the end result of a person's heritage and history. It brings back memories. It evokes moods. That's why food is such a big part of our celebrations and our sorrows. So she feels like she needs to honor the heritage of the food she makes, and she's always searching for people to teach her who are as connected to the food as she is.

For me, to see her cooking is to see her truly happy. It showed as she congratulated the cook-off winners and asked them about their paella process. Her entire face lit up when she talked about creating food.

I studied the way she was able to talk into the camera and talk to the people she was interviewing at the same time. It was almost as if she was including her viewers in the conversation. That wasn't easy for me, being so at ease with the eye of the camera pointed at me. I hoped with practice I would get as good at it as my mom was.

Logan tapped my shoulder. "You in there?"

I blinked myself out of the spell. "What?"

"I said, we're goin' out to light *tracas*. You want to come?"

I didn't know what *tracas* were, but I didn't hesitate. If they were going, I was going. I jumped up from my seat, but Victoria stopped me with a warning look.

After the scene with my parents that morning, it wouldn't be smart to "wander off" again. But Logan and Mateo were weaving through the crowd. Disappearing fast.

"It's okay," I said. "I'll be with them. Can you tell Mom and Dad I'll see them at the house?"

She scanned the crush of people around us and shook her head. "I don't think—"

"Please!" I begged.

"All right." She pushed back her chair. "But I'm coming with you."

"But—"

"You think I'm going to let you run wild in this kind of crowd? Not likely. But don't worry. I'll keep out of your way."

All of a sudden Daniel was at our side. "What's up? Where you going?"

Victoria explained about going after Mateo and Logan, who by now were nearly out of view.

"I'll come along," he declared, pushing us along. "We can get some lovely night shots."

The horror must have shown on my face because Victoria patted my arm and whispered, "Don't worry. I'll keep him with me."

It's not like I had much choice. I hurried off in the direction I had seen Logan and Mateo go, leaving food and culture far behind.

• • • • •

Tracas, it turns out, are firecrackers. Mateo had a whole bag of them stashed at his uncle's house. We grabbed them and ran to a grassy field a few blocks away. True to her word, Victoria held back and kept Daniel in the shadows with her. If I didn't think about them, I could almost forget they were there.

Mateo pulled a lighter from his pocket and set off the first string. It jumped and wiggled on the ground, the little firecrackers exploding one by one, *crack! crack! crack! crack!*

Again, I don't really understand boys. Sure, it was interesting, seeing the thing pop and sizzle, but really? It was a firecracker. That's what it's supposed to do, right? But Mateo and Logan were acting like it was the greatest entertainment in the world, setting those things off. Amazing. Hilarious. They jumped around laughing and high-fiving each other as if they were the ones who had personally strung the firecrackers together. I just didn't get it.

But then Mateo grabbed my hand and pulled me over to where the latest string was writhing on the ground. He laughed and danced close to it, still holding my hand. Well, how could I not dance along with him if he was going to do that? I skipped over the strand of fireworks like it was a jump rope—which is trickier than it sounds because it was wiggling around like an angry snake and spitting sparks at my feet.

Mateo and Logan both clapped and laughed, and Mateo even handed me the lighter so I could set off the next string. I looked up into his dark eyes and felt all warm and tingly inside. I'm sure I must have been blushing because my cheeks suddenly got really hot. I didn't care— even with Logan crashing the party and Victoria and Daniel watching in the dark.

Just as we ran out of firecrackers, the sky exploded over our heads. Even though I knew from the program there were going to be fireworks after the cook-off, the noise took me by complete surprise, and I screamed. Logan seemed to think that was hysterically funny. For about the tenth time that day, I wanted to slug him.

But then Mateo pulled us down, and we all lay back on the grass to watch the fireworks and I forgot all about slugging.

I pulled my phone from my pocket and held it at arm's length, filming us all together. "Closer!" I told them. "Say hello!"

They each pressed their head against mine.

"'ello!" Logan said, waving.

"*¡Hola!*" said Mateo.

That's when I felt it—the zing Victoria had been talking about. She was right; it was incredible, like a firework going off inside me. Energy surged through me so quick and so powerful I wanted to jump and dance and turn cartwheels across the field. But that would have meant moving, and I wanted to stay right where I was.

Logan and Mateo pulled faces for the camera and made weird sounds, and I laughed so hard I started to cry. I was so full of happy, I felt drunk with it. (Not that I would know what being drunk feels like.) I wished I could make time stand still.

Looking back, that might have been a good idea.

The next morning, I woke at Tío

Alberto's house before the sun came up. Memories from the night before drifted around me like petals on water. The *tracas*. The fireworks. Mateo's deep brown eyes. The white flash of his smile in the dark. Our heads touching as we lay in the grass watching the fireworks. The incredible zing. It was so much like a dream, I almost couldn't believe it had happened.

I pulled my phone out from under my pillow to watch the video evidence. The tiny images of Mateo and Logan goofing off made me smile all over again. I wished I had my computer with me so that I could upload it onto a bigger screen. And update my blog.

I cringed a little when I thought about the blog, remembering the raw video I had posted the day before. I really should have smoothed it out before going live with it. As soon as we got back to Valencia, I'd fix it. And post about the tomato fight. It hadn't even happened yet, and already I was excited to write about it.

Meanwhile, I played last night's video back on my phone's tiny screen again. And again.

Outside my window, the light had begun fading from midnight blue to a deep purplish pink. According to my mom's definition, it was officially morning. Everyone else should be getting up soon. I decided to slip into the bathroom so I could take a quick shower and brush my teeth before anyone else needed to use it.

When I opened the bedroom door, I just about tripped over a suitcase that was sitting right in front of the doorway. *My* suitcase, I realized. Yes! I hauled the suitcase onto my bed and opened it up. Grampa's picture smiled up at me. I set it on the nightstand, and immediately the room felt warmer.

And clothes! I was so happy to have my clothes back. I'd already planned an outfit for that day—a pair of cuffed shorts I'd bought at the Portobello Road thrift market in London and a highlighter-bright pink-and-white-striped tee. I'd found the perfect strappy sandals to wear with it when we were in New York, and I'd been dying to put the outfit together ever since. I laid the clothes out carefully on the bed, grabbed my robe (a cotton *yukata* my mom got me in Tokyo), and hurried into the bathroom.

I had showered and was just about done brushing my teeth when I heard someone thumping around in the rooms upstairs. I didn't have much time. Quickly wrapping my wet hair in my towel, I pulled the sash on my *yukata* tighter and yanked open the bathroom door.

To find Mateo waiting in the hall.

I almost slammed the door shut again. I mean, there I was with my toothbrush hanging out of my mouth, in my robe, hair wrapped up in a towel, the zit on my forehead glowing like a beacon. On the other hand, he had a serious case of bed head going on himself (which was actually adorable) and was wearing just a pair of baggy sweats.

"Um, hi," I said, trying not to stare at his abs.

He scrubbed his hand over his face and halfheartedly waved with the other. His eyes were barely even open. Good. So maybe I could sneak by with minimal awkwardness.

Or not.

"Good morning, Cassie-bug." Dad shuffled past us, scratching his armpit.

That was the kind of image I would have killed for on my blog, but not in real life. Not in front of Mateo. I didn't even bother answering him but retreated to my room before my face combusted.

• • • • •

I wasn't surprised to see my mom cooking breakfast with Tío Alberto when I walked into the kitchen. Like I said, she loved to learn new dishes from people who had a connection with the food. I don't know what they were making, but the kitchen smelled of lemons and coffee and baking, and it made my stomach rumble.

Daniel hovered behind my mom with a comb. He kept reaching for her hair, and she kept swatting him away. "Not around the food!"

"What are you making?" I asked. "It smells good."

"*Magdalenas*," Mom said. She pulled a tin of muffins from the small countertop oven to show me. "Alberto was kind enough to teach me how."

Tío Alberto gave me a smile and a slight bob of his head before turning back to whatever he was doing at the counter.

"She *needs* to be in makeup by now," Daniel grumbled to me. As if I had any control over what she did.

"Oh, hush," she said. "We have plenty of time." She told me to pull up a chair, and set a plate with sliced strawberries and a steaming muffin in front of me. "*¡Buen provecho!*" she said, which I think means something like "*bon appetit*" or "enjoy your meal."

"*Gracias, Mama,*" I answered, which means "Thanks, Mom" and is about the extent of my Spanish.

"I thought you said you didn't speak Spanish," Mateo said, pulling up a chair beside me.

"Yeah, well . . ." I picked at my muffin, trying to think of something a little more clever to say. I mean, I could think of things, but then I'd change my mind because I was too embarrassed. What was I supposed to say, *Hey, you looked great in your sweats this morning* or *I really liked lying around with you in the grass*? I don't think so. (Especially not in front of my mom.)

"You're leaving in five minutes," Daniel said to her. "We won't have time for—"

"I'm going to be covered in tomatoes inside of an hour," Mom said, dodging his comb again. "I hardly think it will matter if my hair is done."

"It will for the introduction you'll be filming *before* you are covered in tomatoes."

Mom considered this and then pulled the apron off over her head. "All right. But make it quick. We need to leave in five minutes."

Daniel pursed his lips and shot me an exasperated look. I shrugged. I already knew my mom could be annoying sometimes. What was I going to do about it?

Just as I took a bite of my lemony muffin, Mateo asked, "Are you ready for this?"

I chewed quickly and swallowed so I could answer. "I guess." I mean, it's not like I had a whole lot to get ready for. Mom had already decided the tomato fight would be too "rowdy" for someone my age, so she tried to make it sound like I was going to have *so much fun* watching it all from the roof. Okay, so a lot of the locals do watch from their rooftops, but I wasn't a local. I also wasn't going to argue, and she knew it.

She glanced across the table at me and smiled.

I smiled back.

Useful, useful, useful.

Travel tip: The Spanish are experts in regional food, especially *jamon serrano*, their favorite ham. If you want to start a conversation, just ask about ham.

Mom and Dad left with Señor Ruiz-Moreno and Cavin to meet the rest of the crew and watch the traditional opening ceremony for the fight. And honestly? That part I wasn't so broken up about missing. Get this: They put a ham up on top of a greased pole, and a bunch of guys try to climb up the pole to get it down. I am not making this up. Once someone grabs the ham, they fire a cannon and the tomato fight begins.

Those of us who were left behind with Tío Alberto— Mateo, Logan, and me—climbed to the roof to wait for the action to begin. After Daniel was done doing hair and makeup, he came over to hang with us so he could film it from above. We are so lucky.

"Our job," Tío Alberto said, "is to keep the action going." He showed us some huge buckets of water he had lined up along the ledge and grinned like a mischievous schoolboy. "And to keep them cool."

Just then, the cannon fired. The boom rolled across the tops of the houses like thunder. "Get ready," Tío Alberto said. "They'll start coming soon."

I raised my phone and focused the viewfinder toward the end of the block. Sure enough, people flowed into the narrow street below like a flash flood into a canyon. And they kept flowing until I didn't see how any more could fit. Already the sun was so strong that the roof was getting hot. Sticky, sweaty, need-to-take-another-shower hot. And the air was so thick it felt like I was breathing through a straw. I could just imagine how miserable it must be down below, being packed in tight like that.

Soon the crowd began to chant. *"Agua! Agua! Agua!"*

"This is our cue," said Tío Alberto. "They are calling for water."

Mateo and Logan hefted a huge bucket and dumped it over the ledge. The crowd roared happily. On the rooftops around us, more locals were throwing water. Everyone below was soaked.

"Look." Mateo pointed out some guys who had ripped off their sopping T-shirts and were whipping each other with them or throwing them at people nearby. "This they call *la guerra de camisetas*," he said. "The T-shirt war."

"When do they start with the toma—"

My words were lost in another huge roar from the crowd. I startled and leaned over the ledge to see what was happening. At the end of the street, a huge open-bed truck, the bed piled high with tomatoes, rumbled slowly forward. Impossibly, the crowd parted, smashing back against the buildings to make room. Men who were perched on the truck started pelting the people in the crowd with tomatoes. When the truck was about to pass our building, the back of the bed dropped open and an avalanche of tomatoes smashed to the street.

That was when the real action began. People closest to the pile scooped up tomatoes by the armload and hurled them at anyone within range.

"Okay, *that* looks awesome," Logan said. "What are we doing up here?"

Mateo's face lit up. "You want to go down? What about you, Cassidy?"

"Oh. Well . . ." Mom and Dad didn't actually say I *couldn't* take part in the tomato throwing. They just said they'd *rather* I participated in La Tomatina from the roof. Of course, that was the kind of distinction that could get me an express pass to Gramma's. "I . . . don't have any extra clothes I want to get ruined," I said. Which was the truth.

"We can find something for her, yes?" Mateo asked his uncle.

Tío Alberto threw another bucket of water from the ledge and glanced over his shoulder at us, distracted. "Hmmm? Uh . . . *sí.*"

Mateo turned back to me. "Well?"

"I dunno," Logan said. "The fight might be too rough for her." He said the words to Mateo, but his eyes were on me, challenging. Just like he used to do.

Which means I should have known better. But I couldn't help it. He was making me mad. I hated the look on his face, like he already knew I wasn't going to go. I lifted my chin and met his stare with one of my own. "I can handle it."

Daniel pulled his attention and his camera from the street for a moment. "Oh. You're going down? Should I . . . ?"

"No," Logan said quickly. "Bayani's already filming at ground zero. I think my da said he wanted footage from up here as well, right?"

Daniel frowned, thinking. "Well, yes."

We started for the stairs when Logan stopped and added, "Watch for us. We'll wave up at you."

I wanted to slap the back of his head. Subtle. Just in case my mom and dad miss the fact that I joined the fight, let's be sure to document it.

Logan grinned triumphantly. But if he thought I was going to back down, he was wrong.

• • • • •

Downstairs, Mateo found some of Tío Alberto's old T-shirts for the three of us to wear. I changed into my swimsuit and pulled the T-shirt over it. It was a good thing the suit was dark, because, shirt or no shirt, by the end of the fight everything I had on would be stained tomato-red. I didn't have any shoes I wanted to get ruined, but from what I had read, I'd probably lose my shoes in the sauce anyway.

"I wish I had goggles for you," Mateo said as we reached the bottom of the front stairs. "The tomato juice can sting."

My stomach twisted. Not because I was worried about the stinging juice, but because in three steps, I was pretty sure I would be entering Disappoint-the-Parents Land. That was not a happy place to be. But neither was Let-Logan-Think-You're-a-Wimp Land. As much as I didn't want to admit it, I cared what Logan thought about me. I pushed out the door and into the street.

11

The tomatoes in the street were pretty much crushed by the time we got out there, so people were scooping up the pulp and flinging it at one another. Since we were the only ones not plastered in tomato guts, we became instant targets. Before long, I forgot all about Wimp Land and Disappointment Land and waded into the fight. Ha.

I've never been in a food fight before, so I can't say how the tomato-throwing compares; but there was something really liberating about smashing someone in the back of the head with a handful of slimy, drippy, gloppy vegetable. Well, technically fruit, but you know what I mean.

And slimy, drippy, gloppy whatever is slippery. Once

when I took a step to throw a handful of tomato, my foot slid and I lost my balance. I almost went down, but Mateo grabbed my hand to steady me. It might have been my imagination, but I could swear he held on to it longer than he had to. The beginnings of a zing began to build up from my tomato-squelching toes, but then Logan smashed a handful of glop on my head, and the moment was gone.

Suddenly, the crowd surged forward. I have no idea what happened. All I know is, one minute I was standing between Mateo and Logan, and the next I couldn't see either one of them. The crowd pushed me farther and farther away from the front of the shop.

I wasn't too worried about getting lost; judging from the covered buildings and storefronts we had seen the night before, the tomato fight was confined to a pretty small area. Once everyone cleared out, I knew I'd be able to find my way back to the shop. It's just that throwing tomatoes wasn't as much fun without Mateo and Logan as targets.

Eventually, the road spilled out into the town square. I managed to work my way over to one of the palm trees that lined the sidewalks and pressed up against the trunk to keep out of the way.

I thought I saw Mateo back toward the store, but he was quickly swallowed up by the crowd. Squinting at the sun, I tried to guess what time it was. The second cannon—signaling the end of the fight—was supposed to go off at one. If I just waited, the street would empty and I'd be able to find the guys and get back inside before my mom and dad got to Tío Alberto's.

The plan probably would have worked if somebody hadn't bumped into me and pushed me away from my tree. By now the ground was so covered in slippery salsa that I skidded and splashed down onto one knee.

The thing about tomato juice is that it's acidic. Not only does it burn when it gets in your eyes, if you scrape your knee by slipping on the road, it stings like crazy. I bit down on my lip to displace the pain (it didn't work) and struggled to get my feet under me again. But that wasn't as easy as you might think. Every time I tried to stand up, someone bumped into me and knocked me down again. It was annoying the first couple of times, but after falling into the muck four or five times, I started to panic.

The tomato sludge was at least half a foot deep. If I got pushed down facefirst, I thought, I could seriously drown. I could be trampled. I could—

"Need a hand?" Logan reached down to help me up.

So much for Logan not thinking I was a wimp. I gritted my teeth and took his hand, and he pulled me out of the slop. "Thanks," I said.

He tightened his grip. "Hold on to me," he said. Without waiting for an answer, he started pushing his way through the crowd, pulling me along with him. I tried not to let him see me limp, but I'm not sure I succeeded. We managed to make it to one of the palm trees along the sidewalk, and he pressed me up against the trunk so that he was shielding me with his body.

A handful of tomato hit him on the side of the face, but he didn't even flinch or wipe it off. The red chunks slid down his cheek and clung to his jaw for a second before dripping onto his shirt. "Some fun, huh?" he asked, grinning.

I looked into his face and felt a strange tug in my stomach. It felt a lot like sadness.

And then the cannon fired. It was over.

Logan took a step back.

"That was great," I said lamely. For once I couldn't think of anything else to say. No wonder Mateo had been hanging out with Logan. I was boring.

"Come on," he said. "Let's get back." He didn't reach for my hand again.

Just then, Mateo called to us from across the street, waving his arms. "Hey! Where you going?"

"Back to the house," I yelled.

"Are you crazy? Tía Maria would kill us. We must wash off first!" He motioned for us to join him. That wasn't so hard, now that the flow of the crowd was heading that way.

"There are showers down the hill," he said when we reached him.

At that moment, a shower sounded like the most wonderful thing in the world. 'Cause here's the other thing about tomatoes: When they dry on your skin under the hot sun, you start to itch. Really badly.

Some of the locals had started coming out onto the side streets and alleyways with hoses to begin the cleanup. They sprayed people as they walked by, too. We were lucky enough to find an older gentleman in rubber boots who hosed us down. That took care of the worst of it, but we still followed Mateo down the hill where it looked like the crowd was swelling again near a row of temporary showers that had been set up on the riverbank.

It was so crowded that some people kept walking right on past the showers to rinse off in the shallow river.

"Over there!" Logan pointed to a couple of showers farther down the riverbank that didn't have very long lines. We ran to use them before everyone else noticed them, too.

The showers, we discovered, were simply plastic frames with garden hoses strung over the top. I figured we probably would have had the same thing going for us if we'd have stayed in town. Except then Mateo wouldn't have been able to grab the hose and spray Logan straight in the face with it. Logan made a grab for the hose, and Mateo turned the icy water on me. I tried to wrestle the hose from him, but he had too tight of a grip.

It was then that I heard two familiar voices.

I pushed my dripping hair out of my eyes and turned slowly to confirm visually what I already knew. Not more than ten feet away stood Mom and Dad, both covered in tomato puree. They were cheerfully talking to the plastic-wrapped camera Bayani (all goopy and red—except for his Yankees hat, which was also in plastic) was pointing at them.

Not good.

I spun around, but it was no use. There was no place to hide. I wouldn't even have to look to know the expression on my mom's face when she saw me. And she would see me. It was just a matter of time.

Mateo stopped spraying me with the hose. "Are you all right?"

I took a quick peek behind me before answering. Which was a mistake. Because by then, Mom was looking directly at me. And I was right about the expression.

I stared out the window and watched the hills roll by. My skin still itched and stung from the tomatoes, even though I'd gotten a real shower back at Tío Alberto's house. My insides stung worse. I couldn't believe my mom and dad were being so unreasonable. They grounded me. *Grounded!* Like I was three instead of almost thirteen. The way Mom talked about it, I was supposed to feel lucky she hadn't stuck me on a plane that moment and sent me to Gramma's.

But I didn't feel lucky, because she stuck me on the train instead. So while everyone else was hanging out in Buñol for the day, I had to go back to Valencia with Victoria. It was so unfair.

"This has been a quiet ride," she said.

"Oh." I pulled my attention from the passing scenery. "Sorry." I meant it. Because if it was not fair that I had to go back to the apartment, it was double not fair that Victoria had to be the one to take me. I mean, she was my tutor, not my babysitter. But if she was mad about it, she didn't let it show.

"Did you have fun?" I asked. "At the fight, I mean."

"It was interesting," she said. "And oddly satisfying."

"I know! I never thought it would feel so good to throw food at people."

"I haven't released that much aggression in years."

"Really?" I asked. "When was the last time?"

She laughed. "That's another story for another day."

I would have liked to make her tell me more, but by then the train began to slow down. We were coming into Valencia.

Since we both had our luggage with us, Victoria said we could take a taxi to the apartment. We were waiting for a cab near the taxi stand when my phone vibrated in my pocket. It was a text from Mateo. My stomach went both melty and cold when I saw his name on the screen. I turned my back to Victoria and opened the text.

> **heard u had to go—lo siento—not as much fun without u—te veo mañana**

That's it, but that was all it took. I didn't even know what all of it meant, but I didn't care. It was enough to know he was thinking of me. He missed me. I imagined Mateo back in Buñol, ignoring Logan to send the text, and that made it even better. I practically floated into the taxi. I was so happy, nothing could bother me. Not Mom and Dad's overreaction to the tomato-fight episode. Not Victoria deciding we should "make our free afternoon a productive one." Not the idiot photographer who yelled my name as I was stepping out of the cab and snapped a picture while I was making a stupid face (practically blinding me in the process).

Mateo and I texted back and forth several times that afternoon until Victoria reminded me it was rude to keep texting when she was sitting right there.

Especially in the middle of a lesson.

Victoria left when my mom and dad got home. I let them lecture me about the tomato fight again (really—how many times did I have to say I was sorry?) and then I excused myself so I could go unpack my suitcase and set up my room.

I was just getting ready for bed when Mateo texted me again.

buenas noches y dulces sueños

I knew *buenas noches* meant "good night," but I wasn't sure what the rest of it meant. Still, it was enough to send me to sleep with a smile on my face.

• • • • •

My smile disappeared the next morning when I found out I was still restricted. My mom and dad weren't going to let me go out with the crew for the day's shoot. I tried to tell myself it didn't bother me, being left behind, but I wasn't very convincing. I *always* went on location with the crew. I guess Mom and Dad already had their B-roll footage, so they didn't need me anymore. So much for my big debut.

The more I thought about it, the more upset I became, until I couldn't even stand to be in the apartment with them. So I asked for permission to go down and read in the courtyard until Victoria got there.

My mom gave me a stern look. "To the courtyard and no where else, do you understand?"

I promised, and then escaped before she could see me roll my eyes and mimic her words. Or notice that I hadn't taken a book with me.

In the courtyard, I found a stone bench to sit on overlooking a miniature fountain. I closed my eyes and turned my face to the sky, listening to the water gurgle and bubble. The sun warmed my skin and glowed red through my eyelids. In another hour or so, it would be too hot to be comfortable, so I might as well enjoy it while I could.

My mind kept going back to Buñol. I smiled, remembering Mateo with his bed head, standing in the hallway at Tío Alberto's house. And the night before, lighting the *tracas,* watching the fireworks, lying back on the grass. A zing shot straight through me again as I remembered the way our heads touched. I'd never felt like that around a guy before.

I wondered if Mateo would come by the apartment after the day's shoot. I had looked up the words in his message the day before. *Te veo mañana* meant "I'll see you tomorrow." Of course, he probably didn't know I was grounded. How humiliating! I hoped I'd get to see him once the shooting was done. If I was lucky, there might even be more fireworks . . .

"Morning, Cass. How's the form?"

I jerked in surprise, and my eyes flew open. Logan stood in front of me, his hands stuffed into the pockets of his jeans. "Form?" I shaded my eyes to look up at him. "What does that even mean?"

He laughed and sat down on the bench beside me, nudging me over in the process. "You know, how's the form . . . What's up? How's it going?"

"Oh. It's going okay, considering. What are you doing here?"

"Why? You want me to leave?"

"No. I mean, aren't you going out on the shoot?"

He squinted up at the sun. "Nah. Left behind, same as

you, I expect. Da says it's back to lessons if I'm to stay on."

Stay on? I turned to him. "So you're . . . back with the show for good?"

He hesitated for a moment and then shrugged. "Sure. I don't know. I think so."

"What happened with your mom? How'd you get her to change her mind?"

"I didn't." The easy tone had gone out of his voice, and it became guarded.

The pang of sadness I felt at La Tomatina returned. Back when Logan had been with the show before, we could have talked about anything. "Then what—"

"I didn't change her mind. It was her new husband what changed it for her."

"Oh." I wished I hadn't asked. His parents' divorce had always been a sore subject with Logan. It sounded like it still was.

The silence stretched between us, filled with unasked questions. Finally, Logan bumped my shoulder with his. "I am glad I came back, though, Cass."

The irritation from the day before melted away, and I bumped his shoulder in return. "So am I."

Then my throat got achy and tight and I couldn't say any more. I *was* glad . . . but I also felt like crying. Because, now that Logan was really back, I knew it was going to hurt that much worse if my mom and dad decided to send me off to Ohio.

So I'd just have to make sure that didn't happen.

"Come on," I said. "Let's go get ready for Victoria."

I'm pretty sure Victoria was wondering what had happened overnight to transform me into the enthusiastic, attentive student I became that morning. She must have thought her lecture about texting really paid off, because my phone buzzed at least three times while we were doing math and I didn't even look at it once—even though I was dying to get a text from Mateo. I was determined to be perfect, though, so my mom and dad wouldn't have any other reasons to get rid of me.

All that perfection must have been really annoying, judging by the look on Logan's face. But if he thought it was bad sitting by a teacher's pet, he should have felt what it was like *being* one. Even though I loved Victoria, kissing up to her all morning was making me nauseous.

By the time a knock came at the door, Logan and I both jumped up to answer it, welcoming the distraction.

"No," Victoria said, motioning for us to sit back down. "You keep working. I'll get it."

I sank back onto my seat, listening to the click of her heels against the tiles in the entryway, the thunk of the lock sliding back, the door opening.

"What's wrong with you?" Logan hissed, jabbing me in the side with his pencil.

"Nothing's wrong with me. What's wrong with you?"

"Stop being such a priss. I don't even know you."

"Oh, like you would—"

But then I stopped when I heard the familiar voice from the hall.

"May I speak with Cassidy please?" Mateo asked.

"Well . . ." Victoria sounded unsure, like she was actually considering whether I should be allowed to see Mateo, given my incarceration.

"I need to see her," he said. "It is important."

He wanted—no, he *needed* to see me! I shot a triumphant look at Logan and leaned back in my chair so that I had a clear line of vision to where Mateo and Victoria were facing off in the entryway. "Back here!" I called.

Victoria shot me a look—probably disappointed that her perfect student had disappeared—but she stepped away from the doorway and let Mateo come inside.

I grabbed my pencil and tried to strike a studious pose as Victoria led Mateo to the kitchen. Glancing up from under my lashes, I said, "Mateo, how nice to—"

He didn't even pause to say hi to Logan or me. "When did you record the video for your blog?" he blurted.

Disappointment elbowed in on my confusion. My *blog*? "I'm sorry . . . what?"

He scraped back a chair and straddled it, facing me. "The video," he said. "From Tuesday's post. Near Plaza de la Virgen."

It took me a moment to process what he was saying. He had told me he'd looked up my blog before I got to Valencia, but I didn't realize he was still reading it. I might have smiled if it hadn't been for the urgency in his tone.

"What's this about?" Victoria asked.

"I tried to text," Mateo said. "You have to see this." He shot a quick glance around the room. "Do you have a computer I can use?"

Now I was really confused. "I can get my laptop," I offered, pushing back from the table.

Once again, Victoria stopped me. "Mine's right here." She pulled her laptop from her bag and booted it up, then slid it across the table to Mateo.

He quickly typed in the URL for my blog, and even though I still didn't know what was going on, I held my breath as the page slowly loaded.

Mateo scrolled down past the banner and the show stuff at the top of the page to my entry from the day before. He opened the video and started to fast-forward through it. Seeing myself in rapid-jerk action on the screen made me feel more than a little self-conscious. When the video me was standing next to the Turia Fountain, Mateo hit Pause.

"There," he said, pointing at the screen. "There it is."

Victoria, Logan, and I all leaned closer. It was that stupid van that had pulled in front of the Door of the Apostles.

I squinted at the shadowed blobs near Mateo's finger and shook my head. "What are we looking for?"

"There was a robbery at the cathedral," Mateo said. "I think you got it on film."

13

Victoria must have called my
parents. I don't know. I was too shocked and confused and
kind of excited to notice. Mateo and Logan and I played
that section of the video again and again until suddenly my
mom and dad rushed through the door, followed by Señor
Ruiz-Moreno, followed by Cavin, followed by Bayani. They
all crowded around the table and watched in silence as we
played the video once again.

"It could be something," Cavin said hesitantly.

"I can't tell." My dad shook his head.

"I could enhance the image," Bayani offered, "if I can
access the editing program."

Logan elbowed me in the side. "Look at you," he said,
grinning. "Always causing a fuss."

I was still a beat behind, and it took me a second too long to realize he was teasing. By the time I smacked him on the arm, my hesitation made him laugh. And that made me want to smack him again. I might have, too, if Bayani hadn't started messing around with the video just then.

On the screen, the three dark blobs I had seen began to take shape. I stared as they turned into men. Two of the men were wearing dark blue jumpsuits and white gloves. It looked like they were handing something to the third blob, a man in a business suit, wearing dark glasses. "There," Mateo breathed. *"Contrabandistas."*

"What's a *contrabandista*?" Logan asked.

"A thief," Señor Ruiz-Moreno said. "A smuggler. These men are artifact smugglers."

It could have been my imagination, but it felt like we all got caught in a freeze-frame for a minute. No one said a word. No one moved. It got so quiet that my shallow, quick breaths sounded like gusts of wind in my ears. My heartbeat was thunder.

And then all at once, the moment ended and chaos rushed in to take its place. Everyone started talking at the same time.

". . . call the authorities."

". . . too dark to tell . . ."

". . . the rest of the day off."

". . . could be nothing."

I felt like I was outside the room, watching from a

distance. A strange twist in my stomach told me I was in deep trouble. But this time it wasn't my mom's and dad's anger I was afraid of. If those men were really robbers and they knew I caught them on video . . .

As if he could read my mind, Logan bumped my arm with his. "Don't worry. I'm sure they didn't see you."

I nodded, afraid that if I tried to answer, he would hear the fear in my voice. I didn't think I could deflect a tease just then.

From the corner of the room, Mateo caught my eye. I'm sorry, he mouthed.

I didn't know if he meant he was sorry I had accidentally filmed a robbery, sorry he had mentioned it, or sorry for the drama it had created. It didn't matter. None of it was his fault. It's okay, I mouthed back.

I hoped I was right.

Travel tip: Always respect the local authorities. They do not have a sense of humor.

We spent the afternoon at the local police precinct. Señor Ruiz-Moreno went with us in case we needed a translator, but most of the officers we met spoke at least passable English. The first officer we talked to took my statement with a bored expression (which, from what I've read, is considered very bad international manners), but he perked right up when my dad showed him the video Bayani had enhanced. That first officer showed the video to another officer, and he showed it to someone else.

Officer Number One took us into a small, stark room and made us sit on uncomfortable chairs around a worn, wooden table. "You wait here," he said.

The twisty feeling came back again. Maybe it was because of the silent looks my mom and dad kept passing back and forth. Maybe it was because of the two-way mirror that stretched along one wall of the room we were in. Or maybe it was because I knew I was going to have to explain once again how I had shot the video after sneaking out of the apartment without telling my parents. I could almost feel Ohio's buckeye branches wrapping around me.

Finally, the door opened again and a tall, thin man with gray-specked black hair and bright, black eyes swept into the room with a file folder tucked under his arm. He greeted my mom and dad each with a broad smile and a nod. "*Buenos días.* So very pleased to meet you. It is not every day I am entertaining American television celebrities."

"*Hola,* Paulo," Senior Ruiz-Moreno said.

"Hector. *¿Que hay?* They told me you were here. And you"—he turned to face me—"must be our investigative journalist."

He laughed at his own humor, and I couldn't help but smile, even though I didn't see what was so funny.

"You have done us a great service, *niña.* With the many cathedrals in Valencia, artifact smuggling is an evil we have been battling for years. Your recording may help us to—how do you say in America?—'Bust up the bad guys?'"

This time I laughed. The twisting in my stomach loosened up a notch.

"Can you tell who it is in the video?" Mom asked.

The detective nodded. "The two men in the jumpsuits were easily matched in the database. The third, we cannot be certain. The image was a bit grainy, and of course he is wearing the dark glasses. But let me show you something." He opened the file and pulled out a notebook-paper-sized photo. "Hector," he said, sliding the picture across the table. "Do you recognize this man?"

Señor Ruiz-Moreno's eyes widened for an instant, and he glanced up at the detective quickly. "Could it be Alejandro García-Ramírez?"

"It could." Detective Paulo slid the photo toward my mom and dad. "Perhaps you have heard the name?"

My dad shook his head.

Señor Ruiz-Moreno explained. "You've probably heard of his holding company, AGR."

"Oh," Dad said, his face betraying nothing. "Yes."

"Around here they call him El Jefe," the detective said. "It means 'the Boss.'" He returned the file to the folder. "For some time we have had reason to believe he has been involved in a variety of illegal activities, but we have been unable to prove anything. This"—he patted the folder—"could be the chisel we need to carve away his facade."

"What?" I asked, confused.

"This could be their break," Mom said.

Detective Paulo continued as if we hadn't spoken. "You can understand why we must tread very carefully as we investigate this possibility." And then, turning to me, he asked, "The video is still on your website, *niña*?"

"It's a blog," I said.

His smile thinned. "We ask you to remove the video evidence from your . . . blog. Please speak of this to no one until we have gathered enough evidence to—"

"But you have the video," Mom said. "What evidence do you need?"

"An image is not enough to convict, Señora, but it gives us direction. Now that we know who to watch, we are confident we will be able to find what we need." And with that, he stood, tucking the file folder under his arm. He nodded good-bye to us and to Señor Ruiz-Moreno and was just about to push through the door when he stopped and added, "I would appreciate it, *niña,* if you would not leave the city until this investigation is complete."

Mom and Dad exchanged one of their glances, and then Dad asked, "How long do you anticipate that will take?"

"Days. Weeks. Months. *¿Quién sabe?* It is impossible to say."

"But we have a show to—" Mom began.

"Señora" he said icily, "your daughter is a witness to a crime. A crime potentially perpetrated by a man with worldwide criminal reach. Surely her safety is of greater concern than a television show."

Mom drew back against her chair. "Safety?" she looked to Dad as if he could translate that into something less ominous.

Before Dad could intervene, Detective Paulo continued. "The men on this video will want to destroy the evidence. They will want to discredit its author. It is important we protect the integrity of both."

For the first time I can ever remember, Mom looked lost. "She's just a child . . ."

"I'm not a child!" I blurted. "I'm almost thirteen." Seriously. When was she going to stop treating me like a baby?

"Don't worry, Julia," Cavin said in a low voice. "I'll speak to legal. We'll sort this out."

I probably should have had the sense to be scared by our talk with the detective, but I wanted to skip right out the precinct door. He told me to stay in Valencia. Ha! Mom and Dad couldn't send me anywhere! I was itching to text Mateo and tell him the good news. We should all go out for ice cream to celebrate. Or maybe to the *horchateria*. I was too happy to care.

The adults were not quite as enthusiastic.

"Well, this is a pretty kettle of fish," Cavin said.

"Agreed." Dad wiped the lenses of his dark glasses and put them on. "But obviously they can't ask us to stay in

Spain indefinitely. We're American citizens. They can't tell us what to—"

"That's not what I'm talking about," Cavin said. "We're on a tight schedule for a reason. The show's budget can't take an indefinite—"

Mom stopped dead in her tracks. "The show? We're talking about my daughter's safety, and you're worried about the *show*?"

"We're neck and neck with *A Foreign Affair*," Cavin said. "We may not be able to weather legal action."

Legal action? That was kind of a buzz kill. "The police are going to sue us?" I asked.

"Not the police," Cavin said. "Ye heard the detective. They can't say for certain that the man in the film is this El Jefe, yet they are about to launch a full-scale investigation. He is very powerful and influential. If it turns out the man is innocent, and it was a video on yer blog what disrupted his life—"

Dad cut him off. "I'm starving. Who wants to grab something to eat?"

By the time we got back to the apartment, Logan and Mateo were gone. Victoria said they had gotten restless, so Bayani took them out to play soccer. Disappointment stole more of the bubbles from my good mood, but I figured our celebration would just have to wait for a while.

I went straight to my room and pulled out my laptop.

Dad paused at the doorway, but I was glad he didn't feel like he had to say anything. We both knew I was going to delete the video; there was no point talking about it.

Mom, unfortunately, couldn't help herself. "Make sure it's completely removed," she called from the front room. "Refresh the page when you're done and check it again."

I held my breath to keep from yelling back at her and counted to ten.

"Better make it twenty," Dad said, and left me to my computer.

I was surprised when I pulled up the blog post to see that it had already logged over a thousand hits. For me, that's a lot in just a couple of days. I glanced over my shoulder to make sure Dad was really gone and then quickly deleted the stat counts along with the video. It probably wouldn't help to let anyone know how many people saw the video before I took it down. Of course, since the network was hosting the blog on their site, they probably had stat counters of their own, but maybe they wouldn't be paying attention.

Once I removed the video, my blog page looked empty and sad. I pulled stills from my camera instead and rewrote the post, listing everything I could remember from my morning walk.

Except the part about El Jefe and the guys with the van.

14

Breakfast in the morning was what my mom would call a tense affair. None of us spoke unless it was to ask for the orange juice or the jam. Dad had bits of tissue stuck all over his face from shaving. He'd also missed a button on his shirt, but I didn't want to be the one to tell him, which was weird because usually I live for those things. Mom was all pressed and polished and ready for the day's shoots, but the purple smudges under her eyes showed that she hadn't slept well.

"I deleted the video," I reminded them. "It's no big deal." So why did it feel like I had a brick in my stomach? It's not like I was the one who did anything wrong. Except the whole sneaking-out thing, I mean.

Mom opened her mouth as though she was going to say something, but then Dad's phone rang and she watched silently as he fished it out of his pocket.

"Oh, John. Hello." John is the executive producer in New York who had been pushing for me to be included in more of the show. I held my breath, wondering if he'd heard about the video on my blog. I got my answer when Dad pushed away from the table and walked into the other room to talk.

Mom watched him go and then turned back to me. "Well," she said, smoothing her napkin on the table, "I wonder if it will be as hot today."

Was she kidding? She wanted to talk about the weather?

"We're lucky this place has air-conditioning. A lot of the older apartment buildings don't."

"Uh-huh."

"Do you remember that year we were in Thailand in June? It was miserable. Of course, you may have been too young—"

"I remember," I said.

"That was . . . what? Three years ago?"

"Four."

"Oh, yes." She let the pitiful conversation die there. I guess I could have kept it going, but I was as nervous about the call as she was. I just didn't feel like I had to keep talking to cover it up.

Finally, Dad returned to the table. He sat down without saying a word.

"Well?" Mom asked.

"They're monitoring the fallout very carefully."

"Fallout?" I didn't like the sound of that.

"Apparently, some international news agencies have picked up the video and are—"

"But I deleted it," I said.

He nodded. "Well, *apparently*," he said again, drawing out the word, "other readers noticed the men in the video before Mateo did. Several of them copied the footage before it was removed and posted it around the Web."

That strange twisting returned. "But isn't that illegal?" I asked. "That was *my* video."

"Well, technically, yes," Dad said, his voice sounding even more tired than before. "Legal is looking into it, but there's likely nothing they can do. Once word got out who was possibly involved, there were too many—"

"But how could they know?" I asked. "We could barely even see the men ourselves."

"They could have used the same video-enhancement programs as Bayani did," Mom said.

Dad agreed. "Speculation is a popular online sport. Any evidence, real or imagined, is enough to fuel the fire. In any event, the network brass said that ordering the videos to be removed would be pointless. The cat's already out of the bag, so to speak."

I almost didn't dare ask, but I had to, after the way Cavin had acted like any delay could be the end of the world. "How will this affect the show?"

"Well, now, this is the interesting part." Dad leaned back in his chair. "They think the attention may actually boost our ratings."

"No publicity is bad publicity," Mom murmured.

"Is that what they mean by fallout?" I asked.

Dad considered that for a moment. "Well, yes. Partly. They'll be conducting a few polls, watching the hits on websites and news crawls."

"And as for this episode?" Mom asked.

"They'd like us to continue taping as usual."

She nodded slowly. "Well, then," she said. I couldn't tell by her tone if she was relieved or annoyed. "I suppose we should get ready. We have a full schedule today." She pulled her cell phone from her front pocket. "I'll call Daniel and let him know he can come up for hair and makeup."

Awesome. I couldn't wait for us all to get together so I could talk to Mateo and Logan and tell them about the phone call. "Where are we going today?"

"*We*," Mom said pointedly, "will be filming at the City of Arts and Sciences. *You* are restricted."

"What? Are you kidding me? It's already been two days! Shouldn't I get some kind of consideration for my part in catching the bad guys?"

She shook her head. "I'm sorry, Cassidy. Regardless of the circumstances, your restriction stands."

"Not to mention," Dad put in, "that we don't know what kind of reaction to expect from this video business. It seems not to be prudent to expose you to the crowds that tend to gather around our tapings."

"But—"

"No arguments," he said. "Victoria will be by at ten for your lessons."

Mom was in the makeup chair when Bayani stopped by to go over the day's itinerary. I sat in the kitchen with him while he waited.

"I don't get to go with you today," I told him.

"I heard. Bummer."

"Will . . . will everyone else be going?"

He laughed. "Yes, the boys will be there. And I'm sure they'll both miss you horribly."

I tried to smack the side of his head, but he dodged the hit. "Too slow!" he crowed.

I folded my arms and glared at him.

"Which one are you crushing on?" he asked, teasing.

I swatted at him again, and this time I got him. Hard. He just laughed.

"I'll tell them you said hi," he said sweetly.

I started to swing at him once more, but Mom chose

that moment to come into the kitchen. "That's enough, Cassidy."

Bayani grinned triumphantly. I excused myself and retreated to my room.

I didn't think that things could get any worse, but I was wrong. Since we wouldn't be visiting the sites with my mom and dad and the crew, Victoria put together an historical walking tour for us in Old Town. Which was seriously unfair. At the very least, Logan should have had to come on the walk with us. Didn't his dad say he had to do the lessons, too? But then, *someone* had to keep Mateo company. Logan was probably more than happy to be that someone.

Victoria decided to start the tour at, of all places, the Valencia Cathedral. At least we stopped in front of the cathedral instead of in the back, where all the trouble had started, but still. I didn't want to be there at all, and I told her that.

"Come now," she said. "This cathedral has a fascinating history. It began as a Visigoth chapel built by the Romans nearly two thousand years ago. The Moors replaced the chapel with a mosque when they were in power, and then the Christians turned the mosque into a cathedral. You might be interested to know that some people say this is the very chapel where the Holy Grail is kept."

"Wait. You're talking about *the* Holy Grail?"

"Yes. Of course I'm speaking of *the* Holy Grail . . . although some experts dispute it."

"Do you think that's what those guys were after?" I asked.

"Perhaps," Victoria said. "Although the cathedral houses a museum where a number of valuable artifacts are kept. It's possible those would have been much easier targets."

We continued our walking tour, but I wasn't paying much attention. I kept thinking about the Holy Grail and feeling rather important. My video had led to the capture of at least two artifact smugglers. For all we knew, they could have been a part of a huge smuggling operation, and if they hadn't been stopped, they actually could have gone after the grail. They might even—

"Cassidy, are you even listening?"

"Yes," I lied.

"Then what was the last thing I said?"

"You asked if I was listening."

"Very funny. Now pay attention."

I would have. Except by then we had come to the Torres de Serranos, which is this old sentry gate at the far end of the historic quarter. It was cool looking and all, but she kept droning on and on about how it had been built in the fourteenth century and how the road from the exit led west to Barcelona. Blah, blah, blah. I don't know if it's possible to sleep standing up, but I was getting pretty close to finding out. I tried to listen and to answer her questions as attentively as I could, but seriously? I didn't really care that the two gothic guard towers flanking the gate were polygonal.

"Cassidy." She turned to scold me, but then she slipped her arm through mine instead and said in a low voice, "Walk!"

I tried to pull my arm away. "I'm sorry. Jeez! I'll pay more attention to—"

"Keep walking," she said, tightening her grip on my arm. "And don't turn around."

"What's wrong?" I asked, looking back over my shoulder.

"No," she hissed. "I said *don't* turn around!"

But it was too late. I had already seen the photographer lurking in the alleyway. More to the point, he saw me see him. Which meant he didn't have to hide anymore. He stepped right out into the open and started snapping away.

"Let's go." Victoria quickened her step so that I practically had to run to keep up with her.

"What's he doing?"

"What does it look like he's doing?"

"Taking pictures?" I said. "Awesome!"

"What on earth are you talking about?"

"This is so cool! I have a papa-stalker!" I'd never been chased by a paparazzo before. Not by myself, anyway. Maybe with Mom or Dad. I glanced behind us again. "Wait till I tell Mateo and . . . uh-oh."

"What is it?"

"Um, there's more than one."

She tucked me closer to her. "I should have known. I thought we would be fine by ourselves, without the production to draw attention." She glanced behind us again and then sped up, dragging me along. "Vultures. Just don't look at them, okay? Let's not let them get a clear shot."

We weren't far from the apartment, but she backtracked a couple of times, darting down side alleys and even cutting through a building or two to try to throw them off. I probably shouldn't have thought it was such an adventure. Not if I had known what a swarm of paparazzi could do. But in the moment, I was having a blast. For the first time in my life, I felt like a real live celebrity. I pretended our chase was a cat-and-mouse game, like in the old movies I used to watch with Grampa. I even imagined myself with a beehive hairdo and a big pair of Audrey Hepburn dark glasses.

When we burst into the lobby of our own building, out of breath and sweaty, another photographer popped out from behind one of the potted palms, practically blinding us with his camera's flash.

Victoria jumped in front of me. "Stairs," she said. "Now!"

I cut off to the side and stumbled up the steps while Victoria charged the photographer. She yelled at him in alternating Spanish and English. "What's the matter with you? ¡*Váyase!* Go away! I'll call the *policía*!"

The man ran off, and Victoria lectured the doorman for not keeping the guy out of the building. Her voice echoed up the stairway, angrier than I'd ever heard it before. I let myself into the apartment and waited for her.

"Is this about the video?" I asked when she came in the door. "Because if it is, that's just lame. Nobody around here even knows who I am."

She didn't answer me until she crossed the room and pulled out her bag.

"Cassidy," she said, "there's something you should see."

15

Victoria settled on the couch and patted the cushion beside her. I sat obediently and waited.

"I probably should have showed this to you earlier, but I didn't know what to make of it," she said. "I picked it up at a convenience store this morning." She pulled a folded newspaper from her bag and spread it out on the table before us. "There," she said, pointing.

I just about fell off the couch.

I knew enough to recognize the format of a European tabloid. It's not like it's a serious newspaper or anything, more like the *National Enquirer* back home. But that picture was me! On the front page!

"What is this? What does the article say?"

"It talks about how your video is the evidence the police

are relying on to charge Alejandro García-Ramírez with artifact smuggling."

I ran my fingers over the image. It showed me in mid-stride, coming out the door at the *horchateria*. I was wearing my scarf skirt and laughing, my phone in my hand. I remembered the moment in a flash. Mateo had just done a perfect imitation of Daniel. He would have been to my left. "I don't understand," I said. "This was taken before I even posted the video."

Victoria studied the paper. "Yes. You're right. Remember, there were cameras following us all day as we did the shoot. I shouldn't doubt we'll soon see photos from Buñol as well. Any photographer who caught you in a shot these past several days will probably try to cash in."

"You're kidding." I ran my tongue quickly over the wires on my palate expander and remembered how Daniel said they might cause a glare on film. What if one of those photographers got me with glitter-mouth? What if they had caught me in a really awkward moment like checking out the rip in my shorts or adjusting my bra or something? I wasn't so sure I was thrilled about the idea of being followed anymore. "But . . . why?"

"Think about it. You're the daughter of American television personalities; he's a powerful businessman. It's a story."

I looked at the picture in the paper again. "Is that what the article says?"

"From what I can gather with my limited Spanish. Yes."

"What else does it say?"

She hesitated for a moment too long. "Not much of substance. Now let's forget about it." She folded the paper back up and stuffed it into her bag. "Do you want a sandwich? I'm famished."

I followed Victoria into the kitchen, but I wasn't fooled by the distraction. There was something about that story she wasn't telling me.

Even after the chase with the photographers and the tabloid article, Victoria made me finish my homework. I couldn't concentrate on any of it, though. I tried to ask her more about that newspaper article, but every time I did, she changed the subject. It made me wonder what was so bad she couldn't tell me. And that made me more determined to find out.

The minute she took a bathroom break, I whipped out my phone to text Mateo. I might not be able to read Spanish, but he could. He'd be able to tell me what the article said.

We were halfway through the math workbook when I heard a noise in the hallway. I looked up eagerly, hoping it might be Mateo; but the next thing I knew, the door burst open and Mom and Dad and the entire WIR crew crowded into the apartment.

Mateo and Logan came in last. I started across the room to talk to Mateo, but Cavin stopped me.

"Just one moment. We need to talk. Wait for us at the

table, would you?" He turned me around and sent me back into the kitchen.

When I finally got Mateo to meet my eye, he gave me half a shrug before looking away. I wondered if he had even gotten my text. Or if he had gotten it and told his dad about it. That would explain how my apartment was being turned into a situation room.

But not why.

Cavin had ordered everyone into containment mode. "I want numbers of every newspaper, television station, and radio station in the region. Now," he barked. "We need our response out by the afternoon cycle."

"Response?" I asked. "To what?"

But nobody was listening. Within minutes everyone was either online, on the phone, or plotting around the coffee table.

And I was trapped in the kitchen with my mom and dad, Victoria, and Señor Ruiz-Moreno.

Finally, Cavin joined us at the table. "There's at least a dozen of them camped out downstairs," he said. "They want a statement."

I was confused. "Wait. We give statements to paparazzi?"

"Paparazzi?" Cavin said. "No, I'm speaking of the news folk."

I glanced back at Mateo again. So much for article translation. "I don't understand."

"They want to talk to you about your video. When did

you take it, how did you discover you had filmed a robbery, questions like that."

"They want *me* to talk to them?" I still couldn't believe it.

"You will not be talking to them," Dad said.

"Right," Cavin agreed. "Not here. We should do it properly. Bayani! See about booking her on some of their morning news shows and the—"

"No!" Dad said. "That's not what I—"

"I've spoken with the police," Señor Ruiz-Moreno cut in, closing his cell phone. "They can remove reporters from the building, but they can't stop them from setting up outside. The leasing company has agreed to post a security guard in the lobby to ensure they remain outside."

"We'll issue a placeholder statement," Cavin said. "And then in the morning—"

"Cassidy is not speaking to anyone," Mom snapped.

"I didn't say it had to be Cassidy, Julia."

And on and on. I was trapped in a really bad drama.

I wasn't sure I understood what was going on, but I was starting to put the pieces together. I figured when the network called that they had seen my video and the stats count because they were monitoring my blog. But if that was the case, I didn't get what Dad meant when he said they were also monitoring the "fallout."

Now, according to Cavin, we had reporters camped out in front of our building. Somehow my blog video was news.

And if Victoria had seen one newspaper with my picture in it, there were bound to be others.

So what I wanted to know was how word had gotten out about my video so fast. Was there a leak at the police station? Or did one of the thousand hits on my blog blab to the press?

I left my parents arguing with Cavin and slipped away from the table. In the doorway, I waved to get Mateo's attention, and then pointed down the hall, motioning for him to follow me.

Logan, of course, tagged along.

"You do love to cause a flap, don't you?" he said, flopping down on the bed.

I dropped into the armchair by the window and nudged his foot with mine. "Shoes off the covers."

He opened his mouth like he was going to argue, but decided against it and kicked off his shoes. They fell in dual thumps to the floor.

Mateo took the chair by the desk and turned it around backward, straddling it like he did when he came to tell me about the images in my video. "Did you really get stalked by photographers?" he asked.

I thought of the guy fading in and out of the shadows and couldn't help smiling. "One or two," I said.

"We saw you on the telly," Logan offered. "At a tapas bar. Your mom about lost it."

"They were calling you a hero," Mateo added.

"Why?"

"You caught the bad guys," Logan said.

"Not really. I didn't even know they were there."

"Yeah, but you caught them in the act anyway. That's what counts."

"This is crazy." I leaned back in my chair and tried to decide how I felt about all the attention. Would people recognize me on the street? I smiled, imagining myself with swarms of fans, begging for an autograph. Showering me with gifts. Clamoring for an interview.

"Wait." I sat up and looked to Mateo. "You're the one who noticed the guys in the background. Why aren't they coming after you, too?"

"Cuz he's not as pretty," Logan said.

For once I couldn't think of a comeback. A hot blush crept across my cheeks. Did Logan just say I was pretty?

"And," Mateo said, "because I'm not the only one who saw what was going on back there. Why do you think the video is going viral?"

"Viral? What are you talking about?"

"Have you not looked at it since yesterday?"

"Looked at what? I deleted the video after we got home from the police station. I haven't been online since then."

Logan sat up. "She really doesn't know."

"Know what?" I demanded.

Mateo pointed to my laptop. "May I?" I nodded, and he opened it. "This." He picked up my laptop and handed it to me. There I was, frozen with my mouth open in a small white rectangle on the YouTube page. My video.

"Now look at the view count," Logan said, leaning closer.

I looked. But I didn't believe it. "No way." Over forty-seven thousand views? In one day?

"This is just one upload," Mateo added. "There are more."

"Wow." I sank back against the chair cushions. "I don't understand. Why would anyone care? I've never even heard of El Jefe until now."

Logan stretched out on the bed again. "You may not know him, but it looks like El Jefe is a big deal around here."

Mateo nodded. "Also, in my country, *contrabandistas* steal more than just objects. They steal our culture. Our history. To catch a little one is big news. To catch a giant is huge."

"Yeah," Logan said, "Da says it'll mean big numbers for the show."

"And your blog," Mateo added. "Have you checked the stats lately?"

I hadn't. Not since I took down the original post after we got back from the police station. But now I was curious.

I grabbed my computer and typed in my URL. And gasped. My blog had over three thousand unique hits in just the last *hour*.

I snapped my computer shut and jumped up from the chair. "Hold on." I crossed to the door. "I'll be right back."

My plan was to go grab the newspaper so I could get Mateo to read it for me. But when I walked into the front room, everyone had gone silent. They were all staring at me. No, I realized as Bayani flapped his hand for me to get out of the way, they were staring at the television behind me. I turned around.

A familiar face filled the screen. I recognized him at once, even without his 4:30 A.M. sunglasses. El Jefe was giving some kind of press conference. In Spanish. "What is he saying?" I asked.

Daniel shushed me.

"He says your video is fake," Mateo said. He and Logan had followed me from the room and were standing right behind me. "He says it's a publicity stunt by the show. He's considering a lawsuit."

"Give me a break," I said. I turned to face everyone in the room, as if I had to appeal to their sanity instead of El Jefe's. "I didn't even know who he was until after all this started. Besides, even if I wanted to, I wouldn't know how to doctor a video like that. I uploaded it exactly as it was on my phone."

"Yes, but he's not talking about you; he's implicating the show," Cavin said. "And he may have a case about the video being altered."

"But I didn't—"

"Of course *you* didn't do anything. But all the videos floating around have been enhanced in some way. Otherwise, you can't see who's in the background. Even the video we took to the police had been changed by the editing software."

"But I have the original," I said. "It's still on my phone."

"You didn't erase it?" Bayani asked.

I shook my head.

"Well," Cavin said. "This just got interesting." He pulled out his phone and started punching numbers.

"Where is it?" Dad asked.

I ran and grabbed my phone from my room and handed it to him. Mom, Bayani, Daniel, and Victoria crowded around him as he played the video back.

"Ha!" Daniel laughed. "Gotcha!" He high-fived Bayani.

"This is perfect." Dad gave my shoulders a squeeze. "Good work, Cassie-bug."

"Dad!"

They decided that the phone needed to go directly to the police. I thought that meant I would be going with them, but Cavin squashed that idea right away.

"Too dangerous," he said. "This El Jefe is a powerful

man, and ye've crossed him. Who knows what he might do
to—"

Dad cleared his throat and made big eye gestures in my
direction. "It might be better," he said, "for you to stay out
of the public eye for the time being." His fake-upbeat voice
scared me more than anything Cavin had said. It meant he
thought the threat of danger was real.

I turned to Mom for a voice of reason, but she only
shook her head.

"It might be best for you to stay inside until we get this
thing resolved," she said.

If only I'd known how long that would be.

Travel tip: Personal space in Spain

is smaller than what Americans are used to.

Until that day, I never thought I was claustrophobic, but honestly? There was no place to go in that tiny apartment. I couldn't even walk out onto the balcony because the paparazzi were still gathering on the sidewalk below, and about a dozen cameras were poised, ready to snap my picture as soon as I walked through the door.

The next day El Jefe was formally charged. He held another news conference to proclaim his innocence. Once again, he claimed the whole thing was a setup by our show. It was far too convenient, he said, that I just happened to be out walking when someone supposedly broke into the cathedral. And in the wee hours of the morning, no less. What kind of parents allowed their underage child to wander the streets at all hours?

More cameras gathered outside our apartment building, so Mom and Dad decided to keep me locked up inside. Meanwhile, Cavin and the network wanted the show to keep filming as scheduled. They wouldn't give the public a reason to believe *When in Rome* had anything to hide.

Except for me.

The only bright spot was when Señor Ruiz-Moreno arrived to take my mom and dad out for that day's shoot and brought Mateo with him.

"I could stay here," Mateo offered, "and keep Cassidy company."

Señor Ruiz-Moreno looked to my mom and dad for their input before answering.

"That's fine," Mom said, "as long as Victoria doesn't mind the disruption to her lesson time."

Who cared about Victoria? *I* didn't mind. Not that anyone was asking me.

Mateo kicked back on the couch beside me, which made me smile. He wasn't waiting for Victoria's say-so.

Bayani's cell rang and he talked into it in a low voice before holding his hand over the receiver. "Daniel's in the lobby. He said there's a whole pile of notes and flowers for Cass down there, and should he send them up?"

I jumped up from the couch. "For me? Who are they from?"

Bayani shrugged. "Fans, I suppose. Admirers. You're big news right now."

"I don't like it," Mom said. "For so many people to know where she is—"

"You've seen the media circus downstairs," Cavin scoffed. "It's hardly a secret."

"I still don't like it."

"What should we do with the flowers?" Bayani asked.

Dad looked to me and then to my mom before turning back to Bayani. "Tell Daniel he can send them up only after they have been screened."

Bayani relayed the information and hung up the phone. "We should go," he said. "We don't want to get behind schedule."

They began to file out the door just as Victoria got there. She was carrying an armload of flowers.

"It appears you have fans, Cassidy. Take a look." She set the flowers on the coffee table and handed me a handful of little rectangular cards. "Some of them sent notes."

Mateo took one of the cards and burst out laughing when he read it. "This one's from a secret admirer."

"Give me that!" I snatched it from him and tried to read what it said, but it was written in Spanish. Or Valencian. Or whatever. I handed it back. "What does it say?"

"No puedo vivir sin a ti."

"But what does it mean?"

He clutched his hand to his chest. "I cannot live without you!"

"Okay, that's awkward." I pushed the card away.

Victoria quickly tore it in half. "My apologies. Clearly the screening process leaves a bit to be desired."

"These are in English," Mateo offered, handing me another stack of little cards.

"Good job!" "Hang in there!" "Nice work!" I sifted through the cards and then dropped them on the table. Whoever sent those messages probably meant well, but the whole thing made me feel weird. I didn't know the people who were sending those cards, and they didn't know me. It's not that I didn't appreciate their support, but I would rather have had people like me for who I was and not for something I did by accident.

The doorbell chimed and I must have flinched because Victoria patted my arm. "Don't worry. They've closed off the entrance. No one can come up without being cleared first."

I already knew that, of course, but it still made me tense up when she went to answer the door. I was relieved to see it was Logan.

He came into the room carrying another armload of flowers. "Da told me to bring these up. Where do you want them?"

Mateo pointed to the pile on the table, and Logan dumped his armload along with the rest.

"It's a mess down there." Logan nudged Mateo aside so he could sit next to him on to the couch. "The entire front of the building is surrounded."

I twisted the hem of my shirt. "Maybe I really should go talk to them. So they'll go away."

"No," Victoria said. "It would be like feeding sharks. I'm sorry, hon, but your parents are right about this one."

The walls seemed to shrink in on me, and my stomach went sour. The air in the room felt heavy and stale. And sickeningly sweet. "These things have got to go." I scooped up the flowers to put them outside. At least that was one thing I could do.

Before Victoria could object, I crossed over to the balcony and yanked open the door. What I should have done was dump the flowers and duck back inside, but as soon as I stepped out the door it's like there was some invisible hook, pulling me to the railing. For two days, all I had done was *hear* about the scene below. I wanted to see for myself how much of a mess it really was.

So I peeked over.

"*¡Aquí está!*" someone shouted. "There she is!"

For a heartbeat, I froze like a deer caught in the headlights. Long enough for a photographer with quick reflexes to get off a shot or two. I drew back, my chest squeezing tight, and realized I was still holding the flowers. No, not holding, hugging. Hanging on to them like they were my favorite teddy bear on a stormy night. I threw them down and ran back inside.

"Told you," Logan said.

I couldn't deal with the smug look on his face. I couldn't deal with anything. Hot tears stung my eyes, but I didn't want them to see me cry. I retreated to my room. But not before I saw Mateo shoot a pointed look at Logan.

"What?" Logan asked.

In the safety of my room, I sat on the edge of my bed and let the tears fall. I got what I wanted—to get on camera and to stay in Valencia—but now I was trapped. I always thought it would be fun to be a celebrity. Now I wasn't so sure.

I picked up my grampa's picture and held it in my lap. When I was little, he always knew what to say to make me feel better. He was always so happy. So sure of himself. He probably would have laughed at all the reporters gathered like sheep outside. "I wish you were here," I whispered.

I heard footsteps in the hall and set the picture back on the nightstand just as Logan tapped on my door. "Look, Cass," he said. "I'm sorry. Come on out. I promise not to say anything stupid."

I took one last glance at my grampa. He smiled back at me. "Then you'd have to be mute," I told Logan.

"Ha, ha." He turned back to the living room and called out, "She's fine."

After that it seemed silly for me to mope in my room, so I strolled back out to the living room. The doorman had just sent up a new batch of flowers and gifts, and Logan and Mateo were sifting through the notes, laughing out loud at some of them. Victoria was busily pulling out her books to start with our lesson. The front room smelled like a florist's shop.

I poked at the flowers on the table. "What are we going to do with these things?"

"What? You don't appreciate your adoring fans?" Logan teased.

"Fans, maybe," I said, "but this is too much."

"We could donate them," Victoria suggested. "I'm sure there's a hospital in the city that could put them to good use."

She set Logan and me to work with some math problems while she and Mateo looked up numbers and called around. Within the hour, they found a hospital nearby that would be happy to take the flowers. Daniel and Bayani volunteered to deliver them when they took a break from filming. I thought that would be the end of it, but I was wrong.

Later that afternoon, after we had finished our lessons, Logan pointed to the muted TV. "Guys," he said. "Check it out."

There on the screen were Daniel and Bayani, each

carrying armloads of flowers, headed through the sliding glass doors into the hospital.

"Turn it up," Victoria said. "What are they saying, Mateo?"

He listened for a moment and then started to laugh. "You're not going to believe this."

It seems that some reporters had followed Daniel and Bayani from the apartment building to the hospital and assumed that I was the one who had sent them to deliver the flowers. The rest of the media pounced on the story. Now I was a philanthropist.

"But it was Victoria's idea," I protested. "We should tell them it wasn't me."

"But they were your flowers," she said. "And besides, this is a better story."

I thought about that for a moment. Is that what it was all about, then? Not the truth, but what makes the best story? Those people downstairs didn't really know who I was. They probably didn't care. What mattered was the image they had created for me. They needed either a heroine or a villain for their news stories, so I would do for the heroine slot.

I wondered what Grampa would have said about that. He probably would have told me it didn't matter what the press said about me. They didn't know me; they were only looking for what they wanted to see. In that way, just maybe, the joke was on them.

● ● ● ● ●

I could tell something was wrong the minute Mom and Dad came through the door that evening. Even though they tried to act like everything was fine, I knew better. Remember what I said about spending so much time together in small spaces? Yeah. Kind of hard to hide how you react to things.

I cornered Dad in the kitchen. He was standing in front of the open fridge, drinking juice directly from the carton—something he *never* did. Unless he was distracted. "What's going on?"

"Hmm? Oh. It's nothing, Cassidy." He put the carton back and closed the fridge. "Everything's fine."

"You wouldn't say everything was fine unless something was wrong," I told him.

"It's really nothing. The authorities . . ." He sighed. "Well, I don't understand international law, but it's like you're a material witness."

"What does that mean?"

He rubbed the back of his neck and looked away from me for a moment. Uh-oh. "It means," he said, "that they want to keep you here until you can testify about this case in a court of law."

"Yeah," I said cautiously. "Isn't that what they said in the police station?"

"Well, yes. But this is different. It could take a long time."

"Oh." I couldn't decide if that was good news or bad. On the one hand, it would give me more time with Mateo, but if I had to spend the whole time in the apartment . . . "How long?"

"Don't worry about it," he said again.

Victoria had been gathering her books to leave, but she paused. "If this is not a good time, I can postpone my trip to Barcelona tomorrow."

"What?" Dad said. "No. You go on. This may take a while to sort out."

The way he said it, that didn't sound good. My stomach twisted just a little. "How long's a while?"

"It's fine," Dad said again, though his frown showed he didn't believe it. "Everything will be all right."

I woke late that night to the sound of voices. Not Mateo and Logan, but my mom and dad and, by the distinct accent, Cavin. I crept to the door and eased it open so I could hear better.

"This has gone on long enough," Dad said. "We could contact the American consulate and ask them to intervene."

"That won't be necessary," Cavin soothed. "The police assured me they have everything under control and—"

"Under control?" Mom shot back, her voice rising. "We can't even leave the building without being mobbed, Cavin. That is hardly control."

"Shhh . . ." Dad hushed. "You'll wake her."

"They're waiting for a story," Cavin said, softer this time. "And you won't give them one."

"We've been through this," Mom said. "I will not allow the network to milk this situation at the expense of my daughter."

"We're thinking of Cassidy," Dad added.

"We think she'll be safer at my mother's home in Ohio," Mom agreed. "Surely as a father you understand that."

"Aye, I do," said Cavin. His voice sounded defeated. Regretful.

I burst from my room. "Well, I don't!"

Dad sighed. "I told you she'd wake up."

"How long have you been listening, Cassidy?"

"Not long enough." I folded my arms. "Tell me what's going on."

Mom looked to Dad and he looked right back at her. Silent.

"The newsies are looking for something to report," Cavin said, the only one brave enough to speak up. "And without a statement from us . . . from you . . . they, uh, well, they create their own news."

"What are you talking about?" I asked.

Cavin pulled at his collar. "Well . . ."

"Cavin," Mom warned.

"Tell me!" I demanded.

Dad cleared his throat. "Cassie, come here." He motioned me over to him and patted his knee. But if he thought I was going to sit on it like when I was a little kid, he was crazy. It was time for him—for all of them—to realize that I was growing up.

"What's going on?" I asked again.

He sighed and folded his hands on the table. "It seems Mr. García-Ramírez has a certain amount of . . . control over several of the media outlets. He is using them to discredit your story about how the video came to be."

"They say you're a liar," Cavin put in. "An out-of-control American teenager."

Mom shot him a look, but the words were out. To tell you the truth, I kind of liked the "American teenager" part. The rest of it was just mean and unfair. Still, it was hardly anything my mom and dad hadn't been dealing with for years. That's just how the media is. Sometimes they loved you; sometimes they hated you. It was all part of the game. I shook my head. "That's it? You didn't think you could tell me *that*?"

"There is also the concern," Mom said, choosing her words carefully, "about the danger of having exposed criminal activity."

"Meaning what?" I asked.

"Meaning," Dad said, "that we think it would be safer for you to go and stay with Gramma for a while."

I already knew that's what he was going to say; he had said it to Cavin not three minutes ago. But hearing it a second time was like another slap in the face. I mean, I did want more than anything to get out of the apartment, to get away—but not to *leave*. I especially didn't want to go to the farm.

Plus the timing really sucked. Mateo was the first boy ever to show interest in me. Logan had barely returned. My life was just getting interesting, even if I was under house arrest.

"But they said I *shouldn't* leave," I reminded him.

"Circumstances have changed," Mom said.

"But . . ."

"Cassidy," Mom warned, "you do not want to make this more difficult than it already is." Her voice had taken on a hard edge, so I knew I was getting pretty close to the tipping point, but I couldn't just give up.

"What if I don't want to run away? I don't want to go." I looked to Cavin. "The network still wants to reach kids my age, right? Couldn't we use this media attention to . . ."

Mom and Dad exchanged another one of their patented looks, and I realized that my argument hadn't helped me at all. I had just reinforced their fears.

"Cassidy, you don't know the power that the press can have," Mom said. "The last thing we want is to encourage publicity."

"But—"

"We've already brought Hector into the fray," Dad added. "And Mateo."

My stomach sank at the mention of Mateo's name. And Logan, I thought. I looked to Cavin and saw the defeat on his face. That's when I knew their minds were made up. My fate was sealed. I could almost smell the farm.

"Please," I begged. I was not above groveling. "Don't make me go. I want to stay with the show. I want to stay with you."

I don't know if it was the hour, the shift in argument, or the desperation in my voice, but something changed on Mom's face. She rubbed a hand over her eyes.

"We'll talk in the morning," she said. "It's past midnight." The fight had gone out of her; she just sounded tired.

"Nothing more to be done tonight, anyway," Cavin said, glancing down at the cell phone he still held in his hand. "The network office closed an hour ago."

Mom and Dad exchanged a look I'd seen before. Like they were waiting for the other one to speak up. It meant neither one of them wanted to be the bad guy. It meant there was still some hope for me.

Travel tip: It is acceptable and common to be late for social engagements in Spain.

I sat on the kitchen counter the next morning and picked at an orange, watching my mom and dad get ready to leave.

"We're going to the consulate," Mom said as she wrestled behind her back for her zipper. "Daniel's going to come up and sit with you until Victoria is back from Barcelona."

"I don't need a babysitter."

She kept tugging on the zipper. "Don't start, Cassidy."

I jumped down from the counter. "Come here. Let me help you with that."

She turned her back to me, and I zipped up the dress.

"You're talking to them just in case, right?" I asked.

"Hmmm?"

"The people at the consulate. You're talking to them just to clear things up. Not to make plans to send me away or anything, right?"

She turned and looked at me evenly. "Cassie, if we have to send you to Ohio to keep you safe, we will."

"But you said—"

"I said we would talk." She hooked an earring through her ear and fastened the back. "And we will."

Dad came into the kitchen, still buttoning his cuffs. "You about ready?"

She put in her other earring. "As soon as Daniel gets here."

I turned to him to appeal my case. "Dad, I don't want to leave."

He avoided a direct answer by kissing me on the forehead. "We'll be back soon."

Someone knocked at the door and he turned toward the sound. "Later, Cassie-bug."

"Don't call me that," I mumbled as he walked away.

It wasn't Daniel at the door but Cavin and Señor Ruiz-Moreno, with Logan and Mateo behind them. Mateo had a soccer ball tucked under his arm, which meant he and Logan were probably planning on ditching me at some point to go play *futbol*. Still, I'd never been so relieved to see someone in my life. An entire day of nothing but Daniel would have made me insane.

Señor Ruiz-Moreno pulled Mateo aside. "You boys check in with Daniel if you want to leave, understood?"

"*Sí, comprendo,*" Mateo said. "I understand."

"Are you ready?" Cavin asked. "We'll want to get there by the time the consulate opens at ten, or we'll get stuck in the long lines."

"We're waiting for Daniel to get here," Dad said. "I just called his cell. He's not picking up."

"We should be going." Cavin checked his watch. "Could we call Victoria to stand in?"

"She's not back from Barcelona yet," Mom said.

"Bayani, then. We need to go."

Dad pulled out his phone and hit the speed dial.

Can I just say how humiliating it is to be standing there with your crush and your best guy friend while your parents scramble to find you a babysitter? I studied the tiles on the floor as Dad made the arrangements.

Five minutes later, Bayani showed up at the door, scrubbing a hand over the stubble on his face. "Sorry for the wait," he said, "Daniel and I were up all night going through the footage and then he got sick. Puking all over the place. So I had to finish up on my own. If we're going to pack it in early, we needed to make sure we had enough to—"

"It's fine," Dad said, cutting him off. "No problem. We can talk about it when we get back."

Bayani looked at him strangely. "Okay . . ."

The consulate entourage hurried out the door. Bayani took off his Yankees cap and scratched his scalp. "So," he said, "what are we doing for fun this morning?" He yawned and flopped onto the couch.

"What did you mean, pack it in?" I asked.

He looked at me blankly for a moment and then coughed. "Well, I probably misspoke."

"What does that mean?"

"It means I need more sleep before I open my big mouth."

"Yans . . ." Logan said.

Bayani leaned back against the couch cushions. He settled his cap back onto his head and pulled the bill down low. "Don't you guys have a nice card game or something you can play?"

"I have some in my room," I said. "Come on, guys."

Mateo looked confused, so Logan took him by the arm and pushed him toward my room. We filed inside, and I shut the door.

Just like before, Logan bounced onto the bed and sprawled out on his back, and Mateo sat backward on my desk chair.

"What's going on?" he asked.

I sank down on the end of the bed and knocked Logan's feet out of the way. "It's too depressing."

"What is?"

"My mom and dad. They said we could talk about it, but I can tell that their minds are made up."

Mateo gave Logan a confused look. "Just go with it," Logan said. "Eventually, she'll start making sense."

I swatted at him, but he rolled out of the way. "You heard what Bayani said. We're taking off early."

"So that's what's up," Logan said. "I wondered. Da was up talking to the network this morning."

"Isn't there anything you can do?" Mateo asked.

I shook my head tragically. "You should see my mom when she's made up her mind."

"She's right," Logan said.

I pushed off the bed and paced to the small bedroom window. Everything I did—all that trying to be useful—hadn't been worth a thing. They'd meant for me to go to Gramma's all along. This media thing was just another excuse. And now we were leaving early! "This is so not fair," I said. "It doesn't matter what they say. What they promise. They'll do what they want anyway."

"When will you go?" Mateo asked.

"I didn't hear what Da was saying on the phone," Logan said, "but it's got to be soon if Yans is trying to edit an episode with the footage he has already."

"I never even got to see the beach," I lamented. "Not once."

We fell quiet for a moment, lost in our own somber thoughts. Then Mateo turned to me.

"We should go."

"Where?" I said.

"To the beach. You can't leave Valencia without visiting the ocean."

"But my mom and dad said—"

"No. It's perfect." Logan sat up, suddenly animated. "They'll be at the consulate for hours. We could get to the beach and back before they even knew you were gone."

Warning bells went off in my head. I knew it wasn't a good idea, but I also knew it could be my last chance to hang out with Mateo and Logan.

"Bayani's here," I argued weakly.

Mateo peeked out the door. "Bayani is sleeping."

"He might wake up," I countered.

"We could leave a note."

Logan agreed. "We already told him we were going out to play some footie, so we'll just tell him you came along."

"Which would be the truth!" I was beginning to like their reasoning. "We don't need to say we're going to play at the beach."

"Exactly."

I really wanted to see the beach. But still, I hesitated.

Mom and Dad were convinced I wasn't safe. I personally thought they were being paranoid, but that wouldn't make them go easy on me if we got caught. "How would we get there?"

"Bus," Mateo said.

"I don't have any more euros," I told him.

"Oh, yeah," Logan said. "I didn't bring any money, either."

"I have enough," Mateo assured us.

"Okay. But how am I going to get out past all the cameras?"

Mateo frowned. "Service entrance?"

"We'll borrow Bayani's baseball cap," Logan said. "And one of your dad's jackets. Just until we get away from the building."

"And at the beach?"

"No one cares who anyone is at the beach," Mateo said. "It's the perfect place to get lost."

I hoped so. I sent them out of the room so I could put my swimsuit on under my clothes and then slipped into my dad's room to grab his Windbreaker. Logan handed me Bayani's hat when I met them in the kitchen.

I looked over to where Bayani was snoring on the couch. "How did you get it off his head without waking him?" I whispered.

Logan grinned. "Very carefully."

"Are you sure we should do this?" I asked. It probably sounded like I was asking the guys, but really I was talking to myself.

"We won't be gone long," Mateo said.

"He probably won't even miss us," Logan added. "Watch this." He walked over and stood next to the couch. "We're going out for a little bit," he said in a loud voice. "Is that okay, Yans?"

Bayani didn't answer.

"He's totally out," Logan said. "Let's go."

18

Logan and Mateo left through the front door to divert attention, and I slipped out through the courtyard and the back entrance. Even though I was wearing a ball cap with an American logo and was hunched in a Windbreaker when it was ninety degrees outside, no one seemed to be aware I was there. Which is what I'm used to.

We took the bus to the beach, and my mood lightened with every kilometer we put between us and the city. Until I asked Logan what he wrote in the note to Bayani.

He looked at me blankly. "I thought you were going to write the note."

"I was getting changed. I thought you were going to write it."

We both looked to Mateo, but he shook his head.

My carefree mood slipped a notch. I almost suggested that we should go back to the apartment. But then we turned a corner and there, outside the bus window, the wide, sparkling ocean stretched out before us. By the time the bus pulled over to the curb by the beach entrance, all thoughts of notes and Bayani and going back slipped away. The doors hissed open and a gentle breeze blew in from the ocean, bringing smells of salt and freedom.

It was a perfect day to be at the beach. The water was an impossible shade of blue, foaming prettily at the edge of the whitecaps that rolled in to shore. The sun warmed our skin. I left the Windbreaker and hat on the sand, and we kicked around the soccer ball for a while.

"I'm going in," Logan announced, and stripped off his shirt and threw it onto the Windbreaker. Mateo did the same. I found myself trying not to stare, just like that morning back at Tío Alberto's house.

Mateo grabbed me around the waist while I was distracted and started to drag me toward the water. I dug my heels into the warm sand and held back. "Wait! My clothes! I've got my suit on."

Mateo let me go long enough for me to step out of my shorts and peel off my shirt, but the moment I dropped them onto the pile on the sand, he grabbed me again. I may have yelled and struggled, but of course I was loving every minute of it. He pulled me into the waves without much of an effort. I gasped as the cold water splashed up against my skin.

Logan charged in after us. We were about waist deep when he tackled me. I went down before I could take a breath, so I ended up with a mouthful of seawater.

"Wow, I'm sorry." He helped pull me back up and patted my back until I stopped coughing. "It's okay. I've got you."

I looked up at Mateo and winked and then turned back to Logan. "Thank you," I said weakly. And then we pounced.

I'm not sure how long we were in the water. It could have been an hour. Maybe longer. We dunked each other and splashed and bodysurfed in the waves, and I kept feeling that zing! again and again and again. I wanted the day never to end.

But of course we had to get back before our parents were done at the consulate. So eventually, we stumbled out of the waves and collapsed onto the sand to let the sun dry us off. Next to me Mateo shook the water from his head and raked his dark hair back with his fingers. I sighed contentedly. If I could have chosen any way to spend one of my last days in Spain, this would have been it.

I wish I could say I completely forgot about Bayani and my parents and the whole circus I'd left behind at the apartment, but I would have been lying. I was able to put it out of my mind, though. For a while. A little worry bobbed to the surface as I braided my hair back and pulled my clothes on over my damp suit (not easy), but all I had to do was look out over the waves again and it sank back down, calm and quiet.

Until we went to lunch.

We were all starving after the swim, so we stopped for a quick bite at one of the tapas bars that dotted the beachfront. After the bright sun outside, the place seemed shadowy and dark and cool. We chose a table near the back that faced the bar's wall-mounted television so the guys could watch the sports scores crawl across the bottom of the screen.

Someone had left a newspaper—one of those tabloid things—on the stool Mateo was going to sit on. He picked up the paper to put it on the bar and then did a double take as he glanced at the front page. "Ha! Look at this," he said, returning to the table.

He spread the paper in front of Logan and me. And there I was. Several times. I recognized the first picture—it was the one of me coming out of the *horchateria* that had been in the other tabloid. But there was also a picture of me in the outdoor market, trying on sunglasses. Me, getting out of the cab with my suitcase. Me again, standing on the balcony outside the apartment hanging on to those stupid flowers.

"What does the caption say?" Logan asked.

"'The many styles of Cassidy Barnett,'" Mateo read. And then he looked up at me, grinning. "They are calling you *la chica moda*."

"Should that mean something to me?" I asked.

"It means a girl who is very fashionable."

Logan laughed out loud. "Oh, sorry," he said when I glared at him. But he didn't stop chuckling.

"They say you have a 'unique sense of style,'" Mateo read. "And that—"

"Hey, guys," Logan said in a low voice. "Don't look now, but I think we have company." He rolled his eyes toward the front corner of the bar, where a paunchy bald guy was slurping down mushroom tapas and beer.

"So?" I asked. "It's just some old dude."

"He was watching us," Logan whispered.

"He's right," Mateo added. "Look under his table."

I snuck another peek at the old guy, and I could just make out what looked like a camera sitting on the chair beside him. "Do you think he followed us here from the apartment?" I asked.

Logan nodded. "Either that, or he recognized you here."

"What are we going to do?" I hid my face behind my hand. "We can't let him get pictures of us; we're not supposed to be here."

"Then let's leave." Logan pushed his chair back to stand, but I grabbed his arm.

"How do we do that? He's sitting between us and the door. We can't just sashay past him."

"There's got to be another way out," Mateo said. "Maybe through the kitchen?"

He stood and casually walked back toward the restrooms. Logan and I followed. When we got to the employee's entrance, we quickly ducked into the kitchen. The cook looked up from his cutting board and waved his knife at us.

"*¡Niños! ¡Salga de aquí!* Get out of here!" he yelled.

We didn't stop until we pushed through the heavy back door and into the bright sunlight once again.

I squinted and shaded my eyes. "Now what?"

"We should probably get back to the apartment," Logan said. "Cass, where's the hat?"

"Oh, man!" I groaned and turned toward the bar. "I left it in there. With my dad's Windbreaker."

"Bummer," Logan said. "Come on."

"No. That's Bayani's lucky hat. I have to go get it."

"I'll do it," Mateo offered.

"No, I'll do it," Logan said. "Don't all us foreigners look alike?"

"Well, don't go back through the kitchen," I said, pulling on his arm.

He turned to Mateo. "Take her up to the bus stop. I'll meet you there."

"But what if—" I started.

He waved me off. "Just go."

• • • • •

Mateo and I didn't get far before we saw the old guy again, walking quickly up the path toward us. Obviously, he had seen us slip out the back of the bar and followed us. At least Logan would be able to get in and out without any problem.

"What now?" I asked.

"Back the other way." Mateo turned me around. And then he stopped. "Uh-oh."

At first all I could see was Logan running toward us from the bar, but then I saw what Mateo was talking about. Behind Logan were two more photographers. "Where did they come from?"

"I don't know." Mateo grabbed my hand. "Come on."

He ran from the path, pulling me along with him. I tried to keep up with him, but my feet were slipping in the sand and I had to grip my toes to keep from losing my flip-flops. Finally, I just kicked them off. The hot sand burned the bottoms of my feet. "Where are we going?"

He pointed up ahead to the concrete building on the beach that housed the men's and women's bathrooms. "They can't follow you in there."

By then, Logan had caught up with us. He didn't even ask, but followed Mateo's lead.

"He wants me to hide in the bathroom."

"Good idea," Logan said.

"But I don't have any shoes on."

"You're kidding, right?"

I held back. "Wait. This is stupid." Mateo kept trying to pull me forward, so I yanked my hand away. "Stop!"

They each turned and looked at me. Mateo with concern, Logan with a kind of mild curiosity, like he wanted to see what it was I would come up with.

I looked back to where the photographers were closing in on us. Walking now, I noticed. Like predators when they think they've got their prey cornered. Well, Mateo and Logan didn't have to be the prey. "If I go hide out in the bathroom, where does that leave you?"

"Doesn't matter," Logan said. "They don't want us. They want you."

"Yeah, but now they've seen you *with* me." I thought about what Cavin said. If the paparazzi didn't get their story, they'd make one up. "If we keep running, they'll think we're doing something wrong."

"We kind of are," Logan reminded me.

"Cassidy . . ." Mateo nodded toward the photographers. They were just yards away from us now.

"Let me talk to them," I said. "Then maybe they'll go away."

Mateo grabbed my hand again. "I don't think that's a good idea. You would—"

I yanked it away. "I wish everyone would stop trying to tell me what to do! I can handle this."

"*Señorita* Barnett?"

I turned around. A tall, thin man was standing behind me, so close that I had to take a step back. His skin was unusually pale for someone who lived in a coastal town. Another, darker man stood next to him, his camera already raised, and the old guy from the bar was puffing up behind them.

"We'd like to ask you some questions."

19

I'd never done an interview before.
Without my mom and dad, I mean. So I didn't really know
what I was getting myself into. All I knew was that I didn't
want to get stuck hiding in the bathroom (yuck) like I'd
been stuck hiding in the apartment. And I wasn't going to
leave Mateo and Logan hanging. I was trying to help them,
but you wouldn't know it by the way they were scowling
at me. Like I had crossed over to join the enemy or something. Which was completely not fair.

I raised my chin and said, "What do you want to know?"

The questions started off innocently enough. When did
I film the break-in, did I know what I was seeing, what did
I do when we discovered what was on the tape. But then the

pale guy started to get more pointed. What was I doing out so early in the morning? Why did I release the video online before going to the police? Did my parents put me up to it?

I looked to Mateo and Logan for help, but they just folded their arms and looked back at me. I had said I wanted to handle it, so they were going to let me handle it.

"Now, now," the old guy said. "I am sorry, *señorita*. Luis forgets his manners."

Right. Like this guy was any better. What kind of manners did it take to spy on someone?

"Which one of these young men," he said in an oily voice, "is *su novio*? Your . . . how do you say . . . boyfriend?"

I'm sure my face lit up like a roman candle. "I . . . we're not . . . I don't . . . ."

The dark man said something, and they all laughed. I don't know what it was he said, but I caught one word: *beso*. Again, I don't know much Spanish, but I knew that word from the songs I had downloaded. *Beso* means "kiss." I don't know how it's possible that my face could have gotten any hotter, but by then it was smoldering. I turned again to the guys. Had they heard it? Could they see my reaction?

Logan looked back at me blandly. But Mateo. Mateo's cheeks and the tips of his ears were turning bright red.

"That's the one," Old Guy said, pointing to Mateo.

I wanted to die from embarrassment right there. Except . . .

Why was Mateo blushing? Did he . . . like me? Was he thinking about a kiss?

It will probably come as no surprise that I've never kissed anyone before. Other than my family, I mean. No biggie since I'm only twelve (almost thirteen). Besides, who was I going to kiss? I don't meet a lot of guys on the road. Okay, I don't meet any guys. Worth kissing, anyway. Not that I'd given kissing much thought, but suddenly there it was, stamped into my brain.

"We need to go now," Logan said.

And, surprisingly, the photographers let us go without following. Which should have tipped me off that something wasn't right. But I was too busy imagining the possibility that Mateo could be my first real kiss. It was hard to think about anything else.

It wasn't until we got to the bus stop that we realized Mateo had lost all his money. My guess is it fell out in the sand when we dumped our clothes to go swimming. However it happened, we found ourselves with no bus fare and a four-mile walk into town.

"It's not so bad," I said, trying to be upbeat. "I'm sure we've all walked way more than this before." Although not in flip-flops (which Logan had retrieved for me) and not with angry parents waiting on the other end.

As if that was the only thing we had to worry about.

● ● ● ● ●

By the time we reached the city, the sun was starting to inch its way lower in the sky. Mateo and Logan hadn't said much the whole time we were walking. I could only guess it was because they were mad at me for talking to the photographer guys. I kept saying I was sorry, and they kept shrugging it off. But really? You'd think if it was "no big deal" like Logan kept saying, they could let it go.

As the buildings grew bigger and the sidewalks more crowded, Logan handed me the hat and jacket he'd retrieved from the tapas bar. "You better put these on," he said.

I tucked my hair up under the hat, but it was too hot for the Windbreaker, so I just tied it around my waist. Logan watched me and frowned, but he didn't say any more about it.

Which is just as well, since it wouldn't have made any difference. We had just passed the Plaza del Ayuntamiento when we noticed how people were staring at us. A lady close by whispered something behind her hand to her companion. They both watched us pass as if we were glowing neon orange.

"What's going on?" I whispered to Mateo.

"I don't know," he said.

"Uh, guys . . ." Logan tugged on my arm.

I turned around and saw a policeman at Logan's elbow.

"Cassidy Barnett?" he asked.

I've never been afraid of the police before, but suddenly

a chill washed over me even colder than the ocean. "Yes," I said. "That's me."

"Come with me," he said. "We've been looking for you." And then he gave Mateo and Logan a stern glare. "And you, *guapos*."

Travel tip: In Spain, it is generally accepted for several people to talk at once. Expect to be interrupted.

Cavin was standing just inside the door with his phone pressed to his ear. ". . . has come home. Yes. She's here now . . ." He cupped his hand over the receiver and mouthed, "It's the network. They're happy you're safe." He gave Logan a hard stare, and then he turned back to the phone. "No. I don't know about an interview quite yet. The Barnetts don't want . . . yes, I understand."

Bayani sat with his head in his hands. He looked miserable. Sick, even. He glanced up when I walked into the room, and you could almost see the tension rolling off him. My stomach curled inward. That was my fault.

I probably should have gone and hugged him. He looked like he needed a hug. But I couldn't face him. Not after what we'd done. I hadn't thought of how it would make him feel to find me gone. I hadn't thought what our disappearance would mean to him. I hadn't thought of anything but seeing that stupid beach.

Near the kitchen, Dad stood talking to a man in a dark

suit. He broke away when he saw Mom and me and rushed over to our side. "Cassidy." He hugged us both and then held me at arm's length. "Where have you been? Do you have any idea how worried we were? When we saw those reports about you running away—"

"I'm sorry, Dad," I said. "I didn't mean— Wait. What? I wasn't running a—"

Señor Ruiz-Moreno was at our side. "Davidson," he said, presenting the policeman who had brought me home. "This is Agente Agosto-Mares. He's the police officer who brought them home."

Dad turned away from me and began pumping the man's hand up and down like it was a piston. *"Muchas, muchas gracias,"* he gushed.

The policeman, obviously enjoying his hero moment, responded by telling Dad all about my "rescue." I didn't understand the words he was using, but I could tell by the inflection of his voice and his huge arm gestures what he was saying. And, just in case I didn't, Señor Ruiz-Moreno was translating it all for my mom and dad.

I turned away from them toward the TV in the corner. It was tuned into an international news station that was broadcasting in both Spanish and English. My own image flashed across the screen—along with Mateo and Logan—at the beach. Apparently, those idiot paparazzi had wasted no time filing their stories.

I turned up the sound just enough to hear the anchorwoman report how I had run away from home to escape the scrutiny of my story about the robbery and my mysteriously convenient video of El Jefe. I was aided, she said, by my Spanish boyfriend (okay, so I liked that part) and the son of one of the show's producers.

A panel of "experts" joined her next, debating whether I should be pitied or vilified. Was I a victim of my parents' celebrity, or just another American teen run amok? One lady insisted that I was just a pawn in the network's ploy to boost ratings for the show. Another painted me as a trouble-maker who ran wild in the streets. The panel's psychiatrist theorized that I had missed out on a real childhood because of my parents' show.

I had heard enough. I turned off the TV and retreated to my room. Even though I had shut my door, I could still hear everyone in the apartment talking. Talking about me.

I sat on my bed and blinked against the tears. Hugging my fuzzy pillow, I looked at the photo on my dresser. "I really blew it this time, Grampa," I whispered. "What am I going to do?"

The next morning when I woke up, Mom was already down with the production crew, going over the tapes to see if they had enough footage to pull together for the Valencia episode. After what they called my "ordeal," Mom and Dad were able to convince the executive producers that it was not in anyone's best interest for us to stay in Spain. The executive producers convinced the Spanish authorities. My guess was they were happy to get rid of me, after all the trouble I had caused.

Dad was poring over travel itineraries at the kitchen table. He barely looked up when I came into the room.

I took the chair across from him and stared at the wood grain in the table in front of me. "Dad, I'm sorry," I said. "I didn't mean for it to—"

He glanced up at me, and the disappointment that showed on his face stopped me cold.

I dropped my eyes again. "I just wanted you to know," I said in a small voice.

When he didn't answer me, I excused myself from the table and slunk back to my room.

I sat on my bed and hugged my pillow again. In all the years I'd been doing stupid things, my dad had never given me the silent treatment before.

Bayani had done about the same thing last night. I had tried to apologize, and he kept saying okay, okay; but I noticed he never looked at me when he said it. He just looked around me, like there was a blank spot where I was standing and he couldn't find where my voice was coming from. I guess I deserved it.

And I probably deserved the way Mateo and Logan stopped talking to me, too, but I reached for my phone anyway, to text Mateo and tell him I was sorry one more time. But then I remembered. The police were keeping my phone as evidence.

I wrapped my arms around myself and cried.

Mom knocked on my door at lunchtime to ask if I was hungry, but I just stared at the wall and shook my head. My stomach had turned into an empty, aching hole. I didn't think I would ever be hungry again.

She walked back out into the kitchen where she and Dad whispered about me, but not quite soft enough. It was very sad, they agreed, but I needed to learn my lesson. I lay back on my bed and let the tears fall again.

Mom didn't knock on my door again until shadows were starting to swell in the corners of the room. "Cassie?" She opened the door a crack. "Logan is here to see you. Shall I let him in?"

I sat up and pushed my tangled hair out of my face. My throat was suddenly too tight to answer, so I just nodded. She ushered him inside and hovered for a second. And then, against her own rules, she shut the door.

Logan stood in his spot as her footsteps faded away down the hall. "Da had to come over and talk show nonsense with yer folks," he said.

I picked at the blanket. "Oh."

He took a cautious step forward. "You okay?" he whispered.

I shrugged. "You?"

"I guess."

"What's going on?" I asked.

"Nothing." But from the way he was banging his fist against his leg, I knew he wasn't telling me the truth.

"Logan."

He glanced at the closed door as if he could see through it. Finally, he turned back to me and said in a low voice, "I only know what I overheard. It's not much."

I almost didn't dare ask. "What?"

"Da was talking to the network. There was tell of a lawsuit. Something about slander—"

"A lawsuit? But who—"

He hunched his shoulders. "Dunno. That El Jefe guy, probably. I didn't hear that part."

"Oh, my gosh." I hid my face with my hands, but I couldn't hide the tremble in my voice. "This is all my fault."

"Ah, now don't do that." He looked away. Like it was more embarrassing for him than it was for me if I cried.

"Can't help it," I sniffed. "This . . . all this. It was never supposed to happen."

"I know."

I wiped my eyes. "I was only thinking about what I wanted. I didn't think about how it would affect anyone else."

He looked at me sideways. "Well, you kind of are a troublemaker."

The tears stung my eyes, and I hid my face behind my hands again. "I know," I wailed.

Logan crossed to the bed, and the mattress shifted as he sat down beside me. It caught me off balance and I ended up leaning into him, my face smushed up against his chest. I was about to pull away when he snaked a tentative arm around me and patted my hand awkwardly. "Hey. I didn't mean it. It'll be all right."

"Will it?"

His shoulders rose and fell as he shrugged. "I don't know. But no matter what happens, I'll be here for you, deal?"

"You better be," I mumbled.

"What's that supposed to mean?"

"Don't go away again."

He chuckled, which felt kind of funny with my cheek against his chest. "I'll stay as long as you do," he said.

Which made me cry again.

Logan and his dad left when it was
dark. I stayed in my room because I couldn't face my mom
and dad. Despite what Logan had said to make me feel better, I still had a hollow ache in the pit of my stomach.

After a long while I pushed off the bed and crossed to
my desk. I sat and powered up my computer for the first
time in days. When the Internet connected, I logged on to
my blog. The way I saw it, I didn't have any other choice.
Everyone wanted to talk to me, but no one would listen.
So I had to turn to the venue that started all the trouble in
the first place. I stared at the blinking cursor on the screen,
thought for a moment, and started to write.

I WANT YOU TO KNOW

This isn't easy for me. My grampa used to say that nothing worthwhile ever is.

I've heard what some people have been saying about me. How I shouldn't have been out so early in the morning to capture that video. How I must have been doing something wrong. And they are right. This whole mess started because I snuck out of our apartment, which was against the rules. I should never have been in the plaza in the first place. Then none of this would ever have happened.

Yesterday I caused more trouble because I broke the rules again. I wasn't thinking about anyone but myself and how I wanted to see the beach. I didn't run away like some news shows are saying, but I did leave without telling anyone where I was going. And I dragged my friends along.

The result is that I let my family and my friends down.

I want you to know that this drama is all my fault. Not my mom's, not my dad's, not the show's. I'm the one who messed up. Me. And for that I am truly sorry.

I'll be going away for a while, so I won't be blogging about the show. I'm going to live with my gramma. I haven't really been fair to her, either, since my grampa died. I just thought about myself and how much it hurt me to have him gone. I didn't think about how much she must be hurting, too. It's time for me to make that right.

I've been scared to leave the show because without it, I don't know who I am. But maybe it's time I learned.

Cassidy Barnett

I hit the Publish button before I could change my mind. I didn't realize I was crying until I felt a tear roll down my cheek. I swiped at it with the back of my hand and pushed away from the desk. There was still one more thing I had to do.

"Mom? Dad?" I called from my bedroom door. "Can you come here a minute? There's something important I need to show you."

I slept in the next morning. I figured after my confession, there would be no reason to get up. I already knew Mom and Dad were shipping me off. There didn't seem like much else in the day to look forward to.

So I was surprised when I finally stumbled out into the kitchen, yawning and stretching my arms over my head, to see Cavin and Logan sitting at the kitchen table with Mom and Dad. And they all looked up at me when I walked into the room. Not angry. Not exactly smiling, either—except Cavin. He was grinning like he had just told a joke and I was the punch line.

I stopped and looked behind me. "What?" Smoothed a hand over my mussed-up hair. Quickly felt under my nose.

"Come have a look," Dad said, motioning me to join them.

"You're not gonna believe this." Logan's tone said that he didn't quite believe it, either.

"What is it?" I leaned over Dad's shoulder to look at the newspaper he was holding. Well, tabloid, but still. There I was again. This one showed me leaning on the balcony railing, looking off into the distance.

Cavin was practically beaming as he held the paper out toward me. The caption beneath the photo was in Spanish, so I was still kind of confused.

"Apparently, your confession has made the news," Mom said, sounding about as bewildered as I felt.

My face instantly went hot at the mention of my desperate blog post. I peeked at Logan to see his reaction, but he sat by cluelessly, scrolling through the playlist on his iPod.

"Very good, image-wise," Cavin said proudly, as if he was the one who put me up to it. "Shows you're vulnerable. Flawed but sincere."

Logan looked up then. "Flawed? Jeez, Da."

"Well, that's what people want. They want someone they can relate to. Someone who messes up once in a while. Not some little Pollyanna who never does anything wrong. That tidbit about you sneaking out? Priceless."

Mom gave him a stern look. "I'd appreciate you not being quite so gleeful about my daughter's lapse in judgment, Cavin." But there was no anger in her voice.

I pulled an orange from the bowl on the table and picked at the peel. "So . . . does this mean we're staying?"

And then they did it—my mom's and dad's dreaded exchanging of the looks. My heart did a nosedive.

"Cassie," Dad began.

Cavin threw up his hands and made a big show of rolling his eyes. "Here we go."

"Perhaps," Mom said pointedly, "we should discuss this with Cassidy in private."

"Well, we've made our position clear," Cavin said, scraping back his chair. "This girl is media gold right now. It would be a crime to waste that."

"Good-bye," Dad said firmly.

Cavin sighed. "C'mon, Logan. Let's go."

Logan followed his dad, but he turned before he reached the door and looked back at me. "See ya, Cass," he said. "Good luck."

I had to go into the police station that afternoon to sign my witness statement. If Mom and Dad had had their way, the thing would have been delivered to the apartment so they could keep me hidden. But they couldn't argue with the authorities, especially since they were making a concession by letting me go before the arraignment.

As usual, Señor Ruiz-Moreno agreed to come along. I hoped he would bring Mateo with him.

Knowing it could be the last time I was ever going to see Mateo, I really wanted to look good, but I couldn't decide what to wear. I picked up about every shirt I owned and threw each one of them aside. "I changed my mind," I mumbled. "I don't want to leave my room."

"Then you won't have anywhere to wear this," Victoria said.

I spun around to see her standing in my doorway, holding a bright blue shopping bag with hot pink handles. "You're back!" I cried. Without even thinking, I rushed to her and threw my arms around her.

"Well," she said, softly. "There you go."

"How was your trip?" I asked. "Did you meet any matadors?"

She laughed. "Like I said before, I don't think a matador and I would get along. But look what I brought you." She held up the bag. "Hot off the runway."

I took it from her and dug through the crinkly pink tissue paper to find a soft white cotton blouse with tiny tucks and pleats across the bodice. Tucked neatly in the folds was a beaded necklace the color of a robin's egg. "I love it," I breathed.

Victoria smiled proudly. "I thought you would."

I rushed to the mirror and held the shirt in front of me.

I smiled at myself, and myself smiled back. "It's perfect! Thank you."

"I thought it would be fitting for *la chica moda*."

I groaned and turned away from the mirror. "So you saw that."

"Oh, you're quite famous. All the rags are running features on you." She gave my arm a squeeze. "Now if you'll excuse me, I need to go have a word with your mum."

"Wait."

Victoria turned back to me. "Yes?"

"They told you I'm not coming back, right?"

She nodded. "They did."

"I . . ." My throat felt hot and tight. "I'll be going to school in Ohio."

"So I hear. That could be an adventure."

"What will you do?"

"Instead of tutoring you, you mean?"

I nodded, tears stinging my eyes.

Victoria pulled me into a hug. "Hey, none of that. I'll be here, working hard, waiting for your return."

I must have looked at her strangely because she laughed. "Is it that hard for you to think of me as anything other than your tutor?"

"No. I just—"

"Logan will be traveling with the show now."

"Oh," I said, remembering. "You're going to be his tutor."

"Cassidy." She held me from her. "None of those definitions. I'll always be here for you. You know that, right? No matter where we are. Never forget it."

I nodded.

"All right. Now you get ready. I'm going to go talk with your mum."

As soon as she left, I slipped my T-shirt off over my head and pulled on the cotton blouse. The fabric felt smooth and cool against my skin. I straightened the neckline and checked myself out in the mirror again. I couldn't help but think how different the girl looking back at me was from the one who had arrived in Spain just the week before.

I sighed and held up the blue necklace again. It went perfectly with my jeans. Dressy enough that I could wear it to sign documents at the police station (and maybe see Mateo) and casual enough that it didn't look like I was trying too hard. I fastened it on, but something about it didn't feel right.

Taking it off, I wrapped it back up in the tissue paper and set it aside. I pulled the leather cord necklace from under the shirt and settled the charms gently atop the tucks and pleats, pausing for just a moment to let my fingers smooth over the *cornicello*. "I think I'm on the right path again, Grampa," I whispered. "Wish me luck."

● ● ● ● ●

When my mom announced it was time to go, I practically burst through the apartment door, I was so relieved to get out of there. Mateo was waiting in the car with his dad. I settled onto the backseat next to him.

"You okay?" he whispered.

I nodded. "Yeah." At least I would be when this thing was over.

Someone must have tipped off the press once again because there were swarms of people and cameras in front of the police station when we arrived. They actually had to send out policemen to hold back the reporters so we could make our way into the station.

It was just a short walk to the door, but it seemed to take forever. Dad tucked me close to him and held a magazine in front of my face to shield it from the cameras. Which meant I kept tripping over my feet because I couldn't see where I was going. Everyone was yelling at me, shouting questions, but I didn't understand most of them because they were speaking Spanish. One voice rang out louder than the others. Or maybe I just tuned into it because he asked his question in English.

"Cassidy! After everything that has happened, how do you feel?"

I turned away from Dad's magazine shield. I wasn't sure exactly who had asked the question, but I looked toward the general direction the voice had come from.

I thought of my mom and dad, who cared enough to worry about what was best for me before they thought of themselves. I thought of Victoria and Bayani and how the crew of *When in Rome* was like a big family. I thought about my gramma, waiting for me in Ohio. I thought about my oldest friend, Logan, and my newest friend, Mateo. And I thought about how they all still liked me, even when I seriously messed up. How did I feel?

"Lucky."

21

Travel tip: If you have to go to a government office because of some paperwork, be patient. Nothing is done in a hurry by the bureaucracy in Spain.

I signed all the papers, swearing that the video I had turned in to the police was the real deal. You'd think once they had all that they would give my phone back. All they needed was the memory card. But the phone itself was evidence, so they were keeping it.

"We'll get you a new one," Mom assured me.

And then the evidence desk officer asked me if I needed to transfer my contacts. I thought about it for a moment, but really, I didn't have any contacts to transfer. I mean, yeah, I had my mom and dad and Logan and the crew in there. And Mateo, who was sitting right next to me. That was it.

The guy gave me a pitying look as if he just discovered I had some kind of disability. For half a second, the fire flared behind my cheeks. I mean, I'm twelve (almost thirteen). I should have hundreds of contacts, right? But then I looked at Mateo once again. I thought about Logan. And I realized it wasn't the contacts that were important. It was the friends.

Mateo sat with me on the ride back home. "You really have to leave, then?"

I nodded miserably. "We're taking off tomorrow."

He glanced over at his dad and lowered his voice even more. "What time do you go?"

"Around two, I think." I tried to remember everyone's schedule, but I must have created some kind of mental block in my head since I didn't want it to happen. "Our flight's at five or something."

"I'll come in the morning then," he said. "Around ten. I want to . . . Um. Just wait for me. I'll be there."

The next morning I was up early again. It was my last morning in Spain, and I didn't want to miss a minute of it. I sat on the balcony and watched as the sun came up. Purples, pinks, and corals washed over the *miguelete* tower so beautifully, I wanted to cry. My fingers itched to turn on my cell-phone camera, but the police had it. I didn't want to cheapen the moment, anyway. I'd seen what videos could do.

When the first paparazzo showed up on the street below, I went inside.

Mom and Dad were busy making last-minute arrangements. There were still documents to be signed for the investigators, schedules to reconcile for the show. I didn't want any part of that, either.

My bags were packed and sitting on my bed by eight. Not that I was anxious to leave, but I had to have something to do. Finally, Dad suggested I go help Bayani pack up the equipment.

Logan was just coming up the stairs as I was on my way down. "Mornin'. How's the form?"

"Good." I leaned against the handrail. "What're you doing? You want to help load equipment with me?"

He shrugged. "Sounds as good as anything I've got going."

We found Bayani in the second-floor hallway with the boxes of equipment lined up in front of him. "Good! You're here. You want to help me inventory these so we can get them sent off?" He handed me his clipboard. "We need to make extra sure we have everything checked and double-checked so I will *know* if the airline loses anything."

He left us up in the hall with the clipboard while he went downstairs to find a rolling luggage cart. Logan and

I went through the boxes and checked off everything on the list. When we were done, Logan clipped the pencil to the board along with the paper. "That's it. Think we should wait for Bayani, or go see what's taking him so long?"

"Go see." I didn't want to be stuck in the hall where I had no view of the front entrance. Because it was fast approaching ten o'clock, and that's when Mateo said he'd try to come by. I didn't want to miss him.

Travel tip: Spaniards speak a lot with their hands. Never mimic them.

Bayani was down in the lobby, arguing with the security guard about loading the luggage cart onto the elevator. "This guy says the cart has to stay here," Bayani told us. "I'm trying to explain that if I leave it here, it doesn't do me much good." He was starting to use big gestures to emphasize his words, so I stepped back to avoid getting hit. "I need to get many boxes from up there to down here. How hard is that to understand?"

Logan laughed and pulled Bayani away from the indifferent guard. "Look, Cass and I can load the boxes into the elevator upstairs and send them down. Then we can put them on the cart down here and you can wheel them out to the van when it comes, okay?"

Bayani gave in.

By the time we'd gotten all the boxes down to the lobby,

it was 10:15. I watched the clock, biting my lip. What if Mateo changed his mind? What if he couldn't come? What if he didn't want to come?

I was vaguely aware that Logan was talking to me, but I was only half listening so it didn't register what he was saying. I was too busy worrying that Mateo wasn't going to show.

"And then I thought I'd paint meself green and go as a leprechaun," Logan said.

I glanced up at him. "Hmm? Oh. Good idea."

He slid another box onto the cart. "See? I knew you weren't listening."

"What? Of course I am."

He shook his head. "I'm going to go up and see if Yans needs anything else."

"Okay." I waved him off. I was just about to give up hope when Mateo pushed in through the front door. He waved and I waved back, trying not to be too obvious with the relief in my smile.

"Good," he said. "I'm glad you didn't leave yet."

"Still here," I answered.

He stood there without saying anything, acting shy all of a sudden, shuffling his feet and stuffing his hands into the front pockets of his jeans. "Is there someplace we could go talk?" He looked beyond me toward the back of the building. The courtyard.

I tried not to get too excited. He could have lots of

reasons he wanted us to go talk . . . alone. "Sure," I said, trying to keep the quiver from my voice. "Come on."

I led him through the lobby and down the narrow hallway and out the back door. As I hoped, no one else was in the courtyard. We walked slowly around the perimeter, keeping to the shaded areas as much as we could. Even so, the heat made sweat prickle along my spine. I hoped it wasn't also making big, dark circles under my armpits.

"I have a confession to make," Mateo said. "When my dad first told me about hosting your family, I wasn't sure what to think. I mean, I had seen your mom and dad on TV before, but I didn't know what to expect with you."

"Really." I folded my arms. "You weren't sure what I would *look* like?"

"No. No! That's not what I meant. I didn't know what you would *be* like. You. Not just your looks."

"And?"

He looked up at me from under those dark lashes. "I like you."

I couldn't help but smile. "I like you, too."

He'd been holding his shoulders all tense, and they relaxed a little when I said that. He smiled back. "I had fun, you know, being with you."

"It was an interesting week," I agreed.

"It wasn't boring." He stopped walking and pulled on my hand to make me stop, too. "You could still text me sometimes," he said. "If you wanted to."

"Of course!" I laughed. "When I get my new phone."

His grip on my hand tightened. He was leaning in toward me, his eyes half closed. This was it. What I had been hoping for! And yet . . .

I must have stiffened because Mateo stopped and looked at me weird for a second, but then he shifted so that he was standing just a little farther from me, and he kept right on talking like nothing had happened.

"So if I ever decide to go backpacking across Europe, I'll let you know. Maybe you can come along."

"I'd like that." I smiled, relieved and just a little bit sad. I didn't understand what had just happened. There was supposed to have been a connection. A zing. But when he started coming toward me, it was missing. How could that be? All those times we'd been together . . .

And then it dawned on me. Every time the zing had been there, Logan had been there, too. In fact, I got a little zing just thinking about it.

But Logan was like a brother.

Wasn't he?

He had been once. But then he changed. I changed. Or maybe I just discovered more sides to us both. Could it really have been him all along?

In a flood, I thought of all the times he told me so, but I had taken it for granted. *Hold on to me,* he'd said. *I've got you. I'll always be there for you.*

Except now I was leaving.

I glanced back at the building. But first I needed to talk to Logan.

"Well, I just wanted to say good-bye," Mateo said.

"I'm glad you came."

"Tell Logan I can still whip his butt at goals."

I laughed again even as I pulled away. "I will!"

"Don't forget to text."

We said good-bye in the lobby, and then I turned and sprinted up the steps, two at a time, to Logan's apartment. His door was closed. Without even waiting to catch my breath, I pounded on it. "Logan! I need to talk to you!"

A door behind me opened, and I spun around. Daniel poked his head out into the hall. "Hey. Keep it down. It's siesta time for some of us, you know."

"Where'd they go?" I asked.

"Yes, I'm feeling much better, thank you."

I took a deep breath and forced myself to slow down. "I'm sorry you've been sick, and I'm glad you're doing better."

"Why, thank you."

"I'm looking for Cavin and Logan. Do you know where they are?"

"On the way to the airport would be my guess. The flight to Dublin was four hours ahead of the flight to New York."

I sagged against the doorframe. "They're gone?"

"Probably." He scratched at the stubble on his chin. "What's the matter, sweetheart? Is there a problem?"

"No," I said dejectedly.

He closed his door, and I sank to the floor in the hallway. For half a second I considered running outside and waving down a taxi. Wasn't that what they always did in the movies? I could picture myself sprinting through the airport, catching Logan just before he filed through security. Maybe there'd be kissing, I didn't know. But I did know in reality I'd never find out.

Pushing to my feet, I trudged back down the steps. I guess I couldn't blame Logan for not sticking around to say good-bye. He probably thought I had a thing for Mateo. Mostly because, well, *I* had thought I had a thing for Mateo. I guess the theme for this trip could be "Cassidy Is Clueless."

I had just reached the bottom of the stairwell and was reaching for the door when it flew open, knocking me backward. But before I could fall, Logan caught me. As always.

"Where have you been?" he said, out of breath.

"I was looking for you."

"And I was looking for you. We're leaving. The limousine service just got here."

I nodded because I couldn't speak. Now that I'd found Logan, I couldn't think of anything to say.

A car horn blared.

"That's probably Da." He pulled back. "I gotta go."

"Okay," I whispered. Stupid lump in my throat.

He reached for the door but then turned back. "Stay out of trouble."

He looked so stern, I couldn't help laughing. A little. "That's no fun."

He took a step toward me, trying to look intimidating. "I'm serious."

I moved toward him. "I know. It's kind of weird."

By then I was so close I could have leaned right in and kissed him on the lips. But I didn't. Instead I pulled him into an awkward hug.

He stood stiffly for a moment—long enough that I started to feel like a real idiot. I was trying to figure out how to get out of it with the least humiliation possible when he hugged me back. Tight. And then he said into my hair, "It was good to see you again, Cass."

The limousine honked again, and he pulled away. He wouldn't look at me. Jerking open the door, he said in a gruff voice, "Don't stop writing that blog, okay?"

"Why?"

"I want to keep up with what's happening with you," he said. So he *had* been reading it.

"Logan!" Cavin yelled. "We're waiting!"

"Coming, Da!"

I stood helplessly as he pushed the stairwell door open.

"Wait!"

Logan turned and looked at me. Expectant. Curious.

"I . . . uh . . ." I wanted to tell him how I liked him, but the words wouldn't come. What if he didn't like me back? What if me telling him ruined whatever friendship we already had? "I'll walk you out," I said finally.

"Okay."

We walked all the way through the lobby before I got up the nerve to say anything more. Even then, I couldn't look him in the eye. "I'm glad you came back," I said to the floor.

"So am I," Logan said. "Will you?"

I looked up at him then. "Huh?"

"Da said you were goin' back to the States for a bit. But he said you'd be back."

"He did?" I don't know why that surprised me. Or why I never considered the possibility that Ohio wouldn't be permanent.

"Will you?" he asked again.

"Absolutely." Already my mind was turning, trying to figure out how I would do it. And how quickly.

"Logan!" Cavin yelled.

"I gotta go," Logan said. He gave me another quick hug and then ran over to the waiting limo. Before he climbed inside, he turned back to me. "Write me this time."

"Check your e-mails this time!" I said.

He just waved. The last thing I saw before the door slammed shut was Logan's smile.

The limo sped away. I watched it weave into the flow of traffic and disappear.

"*Señorita!*"

I turned my head away from the voice in time to avoid the flash. I wasn't going to let them get to me. Not now. Not when I finally had it figured out.

Leaving didn't have to be the end of anything. Logan had gone away for a while; now it was my turn. As long as our friendship was still there, we could always come back.

I wandered into the lobby and sat on the steps, thinking about the months to come. For the first time, the idea of going back to Ohio didn't scare me so much. Grampa was gone, but his memory was still there. Maybe it wouldn't be so bad staying with Gramma for a while. She missed him, too. We had a lot to talk about.

When the time was right, I'd convince my mom and dad to let me return to the show. Maybe I couldn't find the words to tell Logan how much I liked him, but when I was back, I'd show him. I'd make sure he knew.

It wouldn't be easy, but like Grampa always said, nothing worthwhile ever is.

Besides, I like a challenge.

Epilogue

Gramma called me to come downstairs and start chores at insane o'clock. Seriously. The sun hadn't even cleared the stand of birch trees behind her house yet. She was one of those early-to-bed, early-to-rise types who thought 5:00 A.M. meant chores, not snooze buttons.

"Come on, Cassie. Up and at 'em!" she chirped. "We have a lot to do if we're going to be ready before your entourage arrives!"

I groaned and rolled over, pulling my pillow over my head. "They are not my entourage!" I grumbled. My voice was muffled through the feathers, but she heard it anyway.

"Well, they sure aren't mine." She banged on the ceiling. "Let's go!"

• • • • •

If Gramma ever read my online confession, I'll never know. She hasn't mentioned it, and neither have I. My gramma is one of those types who doesn't like to "dwell on the negative," as she puts it. She just welcomed me back to the farm and put me to work. To Gramma, sharing work is like sharing love.

She must have loved me a ton. We scrubbed the entire house together every time a news crew came out to interview me, which in the four weeks since I had gotten to her farm was a lot. I guess when you live in a small town in a small county, all news is big news. The daughter of travel-show hosts Davidson and Julia Barnett living on a farm in their viewing area was enough for them to send out a crew. But when they realized *la chica moda*, the girl who toppled an international smuggling operation, was living on a farm in their viewing area, it was time to call out the morning shows, the daytime chat shows, and the evening special-interest shows.

At first, Gramma was a bulldog, turning down every request. "Your mother and daddy want you out of the spotlight," she told me. "And until they say otherwise, there's not even a question."

Eventually, though, the media (along with the network) wore Mom and Dad down enough that they allowed me to do short interviews—as long as Gramma was in the room with me at all times. Which was a smart call because, believe me, Gramma would put an end to any questioning if the journalist so much as stepped one toe out of line.

"No personal questions," she warned them. "Nothing leading. Don't even think about using statements from her blog without permission."

She was so tough, I was surprised anyone even wanted to interview me anymore. But they did—we'd had crews in the house at least ten times in the last three weeks. Gramma made us scrub the place spotless every time, so I was pretty sure today's visit didn't require a 5:00 A.M. wakeup call.

And before you say it, I know, I know. This whole thing started because I couldn't sleep, and now I couldn't drag myself out of bed. But that was a different time zone. A different motivation.

Besides, now I was spending hours almost every night on the computer, talking to Logan online. I wasn't getting to bed as early as I used to. But Gramma didn't know that.

"Come on, sweetie!" she called. "You can't hoot with the owls at night and soar with the eagles in the morning!"

Or maybe she did.

Whenever we'd stay at Gramma and Grampa's place, I got to sleep in my mom's old room. I would often lie in her bed and wonder what it had been like for her, growing up on the farm. When I'd asked her, she told me that when she was my age, it was more of a working farm, with a huge garden to tend and cows to milk and sheep to shear. Grampa had even toyed with keeping llamas for a while. But that's not what I'd meant. I wanted to know what it was like growing up with Gramma.

Maybe it wasn't fair, but since Grampa had always been the one with the jokes and the peppermint candies in his pocket, I had always gravitated toward him. Gramma scared me a little bit.

"She never let me get away with anything," Mom had told me, "that's for sure."

Gramma was what Grampa used to call a "no-nonsense, hardworking kinda gal." She expected the same hard work and no nonsense from everyone.

"You just have to get to know her soft side," Mom had said. "She does have one, you know."

"Cassidy!" Gramma knocked on the stairway wall. "Don't make me come up and get you!"

She would, too. I knew that from experience. "I'm coming!" I yelled; and because I knew she would be listening for sounds of life before she'd give up, I pushed the covers back and sat up, bouncing just a little so she'd be sure to hear the bed creak.

I was learning that Gramma's soft side only looks like it has hard edges. Like when she would bark at me to get out of bed or when she'd stare a nosy reporter down. She seemed tough on the outside, but she was only showing that she loved me.

I found out that she liked to put her feet up, too. Don't laugh—it was something of a revelation to me. In all the times we'd stayed at the farm, all I ever remembered was Gramma working, working, working. I could hear her cooking breakfast before we got up in the morning, or running the washing machine after we went to bed. I wasn't even completely sure she ever slept.

But now that it was just the two of us, she liked to spend evenings relaxing. We'd read books or play canasta, or, if I was really lucky, watch TV.

You'd think with a daughter who made her living on television, Gramma would have watched more of it, but she never saw the value in it, she said. Except for my mom and dad's show.

When in Rome came on Thursday evenings in Ohio, so I always knew we'd spend those evenings with a bowl of popcorn in front of the TV.

"Turn it up!" she'd say as soon as Mom came on screen. Or "Is this the episode you're in, dear?"

I had to explain to her every time that the shows were scheduled months in advance. The Spain episode taped in August wouldn't air until October. But still she anticipated it every week.

● ● ● ● ●

When I realized it had gotten quiet downstairs, I jumped out of bed and pulled on my sweats. Eventually, Gramma would stop asking for help, and then she'd go and tackle a job by herself. The only thing I hated more than scrubbing the baseboards was the guilt of knowing Gramma had been on her knees scrubbing the baseboards because I was too slow to get to it.

I trudged down the stairs without even brushing my hair. It was dark (why hadn't Gramma turned on the lights? weird . . .), and I had to feel along the wall for the light switch.

"Gramma?" I called. "Gramma?"

She must have gone out to milk the cow. Yeah, she only had one by then. Which meant we didn't have one of those handy milking machines. We milked by hand, and can I just say . . . ick?

Finally, I found the switch and turned on the lights and—

"Surprise!"

Mom and Dad stood in front of me with their arms outstretched. As soon as I recovered from my shock, I jumped into them. "How did you . . . ? When did you . . . ? I thought you were in Malta."

"We finished shooting early," Mom said. "We wanted to surprise you."

"We've missed you so much, Cassie-bug," Dad added, stroking my hair. "It hasn't been the same without you."

"Does that mean I can come back with you?" I blurted it out before it dawned on me that I might be hurting Gramma's feelings. "I mean . . . uh . . . I'm sorry."

"I understand," she said. "A child needs her parents."

Mom and Dad exchanged one of their annoying meaningful glances.

"Well . . ." Mom began.

"We need to talk," Dad said.

Gramma ushered us into her kitchen. I've always liked Gramma's kitchen. My mom's a chef, and I think Gramma's kitchen must be where she got her love for food. Because with Gramma, food was another way of showing love.

She gave us all steaming mugs of hot cocoa, pulled out her cast-iron aebelskiver pan, and set about making breakfast, humming to herself as if the rest of us weren't there. Gramma always made aebelskivers for our homecoming breakfasts. They're little Danish pancakes that are shaped like balls, and they always remind me of the farm.

Mom watched her for a while and then turned to me.

"How have you been enjoying your time here?" Mom asked.

I sipped my cocoa before answering. I'd been enjoying it fine, even if I would rather have been with them and Logan. I was glad for the time I'd had with Gramma, but I'm not going to lie—after jetting around the world, life on a farm is, well . . . slow. I glanced to where Gramma was humming at the stove. "It's been great," I said.

"Would you be terribly sad to leave for a bit?" Dad asked.

I sat up straighter and tried to hide the excitement in my voice when I asked, "What are you talking about?"

"Well," Mom said, "it seems you've become quite popular."

Dad nodded. "The producers informed us that we get more hits on the *When in Rome* website through searches for your name than through all other searches. Combined."

Okay. I had to admit that was pretty cool. But . . . so?

Mom cleared her throat. "They've been talking to us for the past few weeks . . ."

"Lecturing us is more like it," Dad put in.

"And they would like us to consider bringing you back to the show. As an active participant."

I took another sip of my hot cocoa to hide my smile. The active-participant part was great, but my smile was for Logan. He said he'd be staying with his dad for a while, which meant he'd be traveling with the show, too. I felt like jumping up and down. Singing. Dancing. But I simply said, "I'd like that."

"Glad to hear it," Dad said. "Because the network has a special assignment for you. A kids' travel special."

He and Mom exchanged a look again.

"How would you like to go to Greece?"

Turn the page for a peek at

LIGHTS, CAMERA,
CASSIDY

episode two:
Paparazzi

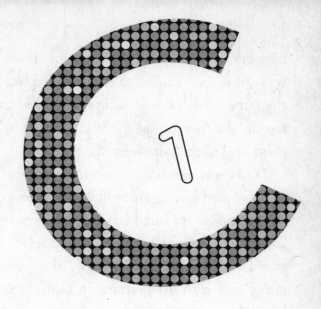

A sign on the wall in the Athens

airport said, GREECE WELCOMES A NEW MYTH. YOURS.

I had to stop and take a picture of it because it fit my situation so well. Arriving in Greece, I felt like I was actually stepping into an adventure of mythical proportions.

My mom and dad host a popular television travel show called *When in Rome*, and I've been all over the world with them, but this was the first time I was traveling on my own. Or at least without them. I did have my tutor, Victoria, with me. It was the only way they would let me go. And by "only way," I mean it was one of a long list of rules and conditions.

My mom and dad's network had invited me to help host a travel special on Greece that would air on their sister kids' network. The only problem was, my mom and dad's show was already scheduled to shoot in Papua, New Guinea, at the same time. They wouldn't have even considered letting me do the Greece special if it wasn't for Victoria. And a good deal of pressure from the network.

They wanted to cash in on the surge of publicity *When in Rome* had gotten since our recent visit to Spain. Without intending to, I had landed myself in trouble there, and landed on the front pages of the tabloids in the process. The attention got a little too intense, so my mom and dad sent me to stay with my gramma in Ohio to get me out of the spotlight and let things settle down.

It didn't work. Newspaper and television reporters swarmed Gramma's farm. I probably did more interviews in the few weeks I was there than my mom and dad did in a year. Our executive director, Cavin, insisted that they should take advantage of my name recognition instead of hiding me away. Finally, my mom and dad gave in when I was invited to do the special.

Thinking about Cavin made me think about his son, Logan, and that made my stomach flip. At one time, Logan had been my best friend. When we were kids, he used to travel on location with the show just like I did. We hung out together all the time. And then Logan's mom made him go back to live with her in Ireland. I didn't see him for over two years, until—without any warning—he came back to the show when we were in Spain.

And I realized I liked him.

I mean, really *liked* him.

And the way he came looking for me before he left Spain, I had a feeling that he liked me, too.

We'd been meeting online to chat as often as we could since then, and things had just started to get interesting when I was invited to come to Greece.

I closed my eyes and remembered Logan's smile. His green eyes, fringed with black lashes. His Irish accent and the way he let his words lilt up at the end of a sentence. I sighed.

"Are you feeling quite all right?" Victoria asked.

By then we were standing in the long immigration line, waiting to be processed.

"I'm good," I told her, even though my stomach felt like it had been inhabited by a vicious breed of attack butterflies. *Excitement*, I told myself, even though I knew it was much more than that.

If I ever wanted to return to my parents' show—and be with Logan again—I had to prove to them that I could keep out of trouble. That I could be an asset. A lot was riding on this trip. What if I wasn't up to the challenge?

Suddenly, I felt claustrophobic in the long line of people. Like I couldn't breathe.

"Actually," I told Victoria, "I think I need to go to the restroom." Anywhere to get away from the crowd for a moment. I had to pull myself together.

She glanced at her watch. "Can it wait until we get to baggage claim? The producers said they would be sending a driver to pick us up, and I'm afraid we'll keep him waiting if we lose our place in line now."

"You stay," I said. "Save our spot. I'll be right back." I didn't wait for her to say no, but sprinted to the nearest bathroom.

You are la chica moda, I told my image in the mirror. *You can do this.*

La chica moda, in case you didn't know, is the nickname the tabloids in Spain gave me. It means "the fashionable girl." And I swear, it's not something I thought a whole lot about before Spain. Fashion, I mean. I just wore what I liked. But since I pick up clothes from all over the world and have developed what the papers called my own "sense of style," they seemed to think it was newsworthy. Once I was already in the news, that is.

That kind of a nickname can become a burden. I mean, it's a lot to live up to, right? I try not to think about it, but it's there in the back of my mind, ready to pounce whenever my confidence slips.

Of course, my mom's quick tutorial on how to behave like a television personality didn't help much. "You never know when someone will be watching," she told me before I left for Greece. "Or when your picture might be taken. Remember that whenever we are in the public eye, we are always *on*."

Thanks so much, Mom. Way to make me perpetually self-conscious.

I splashed my face with water and stared at myself in the mirror. I hardly even recognized the girl who stared back. My eyes looked bluer that usual. Bright, eager. My cheeks flushed pink with anticipation. I usually straightened my blonde hair, but I'd left my straightener at home this trip on the advice of the makeup guy with my mom and dad's show.

"You've got naturally wavy hair," Daniel had said. "You don't want to fight the humidity in Greece by trying to straighten it all the time. Remember, natural is your friend."

Taking a deep breath, I repeated the affirmations that had been my mantra from the moment I left Cleveland. I could show my mom and dad. I could be *on*. I could be a star. I set my sunglasses on top of my head and tossed my natural waves and stared down the girl in the mirror. "Let's do this thing."

I saw the sign with my name on it the minute we rolled our luggage out of the customs area. It's the first time I've seen a driver holding up *my* name. Usually, it's my mom's or dad's name on the placard. A little thrill rippled through me and I nudged Victoria. "Look!" I whispered.

Holding the sign was a tall man in a black suit and a crisp white shirt. He had dark, wavy hair and even darker eyes that watched the passengers coming through the entry.

Our driver, I guessed. He must have recognized me—or at least saw the way I reacted to the sign he was holding—because he tucked the sign under his arm and waved us over.

"Miss Cassidy, Miss Victoria," he said. "I am Magus Demetriou. *Kalos irthate stin Ellada.* Welcome to Greece." His voice was big and deep, just like he was. Seriously. Besides being tall, the guy had thick, wide shoulders and a solid-looking build beneath his suit. He looked more like a bodyguard than a driver.

"Mr. Kouropoulos asked that I bring you to the yacht directly," he said, giving a little nod first to me, and then to Victoria.

Oh, did I mention that part of the deal with the travel special was that we would be sailing around the Greek islands on a movie star's yacht? Yeah. It's a rough life, but I'm willing to make the sacrifice.

"Is it far to the harbor?" I asked.

"Perhaps far for some, not so far for others." He smiled in a way that made me wonder if he was joking or giving me some kind of riddle or what.

Which meant I had no idea how to respond. All I could come up with was, "Oh," and that didn't quite have the star quality I was going for.

But then, he probably didn't even hear the answer anyway. He was already in motion, taking the luggage cart from Victoria and motioning with his head for us to follow him.

"I trust your flight was pleasant?" he said over his shoulder.

"It was really nice," I said. "Thank you."

He led us outside through a pair of sliding-glass doors. I squinted in the bright Mediterranean sunshine and pulled the sunglasses off the top of my head, but stopped short of putting them on. Right in front of us, a sleek white limousine with tinted-glass windows idled near the loading-zone curb. I barely had time to wonder if some big celebrity was flying into Athens that afternoon before Magus stepped up to pay the uniformed attendant and I realized the limo was for us. Niiice.

We sometimes got limousine service when I traveled with my mom and dad, but I wasn't expecting it for just me. Well, me and Victoria. I settled the sunglasses onto my nose and slipped my cell phone from my pocket to take a quick picture to post on my blog. And to show Logan how the network was rolling out the red carpet for this show. Not bad for my first gig.

The attendant scurried to load our luggage into the trunk of the limousine while Magus opened the backseat door for Victoria and me. I slid gracefully onto the cool, buttery-soft leather seats inside, *feeling* like a star. Now all I had to do for the next week and a half was *act* like one.

"Miss Cassidy," Magus said as we wove slowly through the traffic surrounding the city, "You asked how long it would take to reach the port. As you can see, it could be a while, by the clock."

I leaned forward in my seat to hear him better. "You said it could be long for some, and not so long for others. What did you mean?"

"Ah. You were listening. Are you a student of philosophy, Miss Cassidy?"

Victoria leaned forward then, too. If there was anything she loved, it was a "teaching moment." It sounded like she and Magus were made from the same mold. "Philosophy," Victoria told me, "means 'love of wisdom.' A good many of the world's great philosophers were Greek."

"That is right," Magus said, pleased. "Philosophy teaches us how to look at the world and find truth. In this instance, we see that we are stuck in traffic. Does this make our journey longer?"

His eyes met mine in the rearview mirror as he waited for my answer. "Not if you're talking about distance," I said. "I'm guessing it takes more time, though."

"But what is time?" he asked.

Again, he waited for an answer. "Um. I don't know?"

"Protagoras tells us that man is the measure of all things. Do you know what this means?"

When I didn't answer, Victoria chimed in. "Things are as we say they are."

"So . . ." I said, trying to follow the logic. "If I say the trip is long, it's long, and if I say it's short, it's short—even if it takes the same hour either way?" You tell me. Does that make any sense? I didn't think so.

But Magus said, "Yes."

And Victoria said, "Exactly."

And I wondered if philosophy was like one of those jokes that wasn't supposed to make sense, but people laughed anyway.

However you looked at it, before too long, we reached the port. I watched through the window for a glimpse of the yacht as the limousine rolled to a stop.

"Oh, my gosh," I breathed. "Look at that."

Victoria leaned over to look out my side. She didn't say anything, but I could feel her next to me as she suddenly went rigid—not on account of the yacht, but because of what stood between us and the yacht.

On the dock, maybe two dozen people shouted and pushed and waved at us from behind sawhorse barricades. A couple of burly-looking security guards were holding them back or I'm pretty sure they would have rushed the limousine.

Victoria tapped Magus on the shoulder. "What is all this?" she asked. Her voice had gone as stiff as her posture.

Magus shrugged one huge shoulder. "Not to worry; they simply wish to see you." He killed the engine and unbuckled his seat belt.

I realized how well the limousine's soundproofing

worked when he pushed his door open, and voices swirled in with the clean saltwater smell of the sea.

"It's her!"

"Miss Barnett!"

"Over here!"

Magus climbed out of the car and closed his door firmly behind him, muffling the words once more.

I watched the crowd for a moment, then turned to Victoria, practically bouncing in my seat. "Can you believe all these people are here to see me?"

"Well, of course," she said drily. "You are quite a star." She smiled when she said it, but I didn't miss the way she watched out the window. Guarded. Wary. And I had a pretty good idea I knew why.

Victoria and I had been stalked by some aggressive paparazzi in Spain. She was probably thinking about how they chased us through the streets of Valencia, right into the lobby of our hotel. But this was different. There were barricades. Guards holding the paparazzi back. And besides, it's not like they were going to be able to chase after us as we got onto the yacht.

When Magus opened the back door for us, the voices rushed in again. Calling my name. Calling for *me*. I forgot all about Victoria and her hesitation and stepped out into the warmth of sunlight and admiration.

The crowd pressed forward. *My* crowd. I waved to them

the way I had seen my mom and dad do a million times, pausing to make eye contact with a couple of the photographers long enough to let them get a good shot. Mom always said you had to control your image.

"Right, Miss Diva," Victoria said. Her smile was a little more relaxed as she slipped her arm through mine and turned me away from the cameras. "Let's get you on that boat."

"It's a yacht," I sniffed.

She laughed, but really? I was being serious. We were about to be hosted by one of Greece's biggest movie stars, and the word *boat* didn't quite convey the appropriate glamour of the situation. Besides, even *yacht* was an understatement for the *Pandora*. She was practically a ship, long and sleek and glistening white against a backdrop of cobalt-blue water. Her name was painted in both Greek and Roman lettering on the bow. A crimson-carpeted gangplank stretched up from the pier to the deck. (Ha. I was right about rolling out the red carpet.) As soon as our backs were turned to the paparazzi, I snuck a quick photo of the *Pandora* for my blog.

My heart skipped a beat as I let my eyes follow the gangplank's path to where our movie-star host and his son were waiting to greet us. I'd seen pictures of both of them online, but none of the photos even came close to the real thing.

Nikos Kouropolous—who, from what I had read in his

online bio, was only about five months older than me—had heavy Mediterranean brows and thick, dark hair, his short curls ruffling in the breeze.

His father, Constantine Kouropoulos, probably once had the same dark curls as Nikos, but now his hair was streaked with silver. He wore it brushed straight back from his forehead. Very cosmopolitan, even if I thought it was a little severe.

But I wasn't exactly giving Mr. Kouropolos or his hair much thought at that moment. I poked Victoria. "That's him!" I whispered. "That's Nikos."

ISBN: 978-0-14-241816-1

Cassidy is thrilled when the time comes for her and Logan to start filming publicity spots for their parents' TV show in Costa Rica. But there's a damper on her sunshiny outlook when she discovers that someone hacked into her blog and is posting some pretty negative things—jeopardizing her whole role on the show. Can Cassidy enlist Logan's help and figure out what's going on—before it's lights out for Lights, Camera, Cassidy?

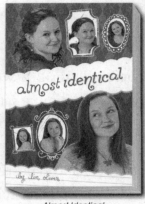